MW00573761

Praise for *Jamaica Ginger and Other Concoctions*

★ "A commanding short-story collection, Caribbean Canadian Nalo Hopkinson's *Jamaica Ginger and Other Concoctions* blends ecological awareness, cultural heritage, and fantastical happenings. . . . Climate change is a recurring theme: There are diseased, parched landscapes and ravaging floods. Many of the characters are resourceful women of color who are determined to improve their troubled environments; they summon remarkable scientific, technological, and mechanical abilities to heal others and solve problems. Enriched with a marrow of emotion, the short stories of *Jamaica Ginger and Other Concoctions* move beyond bleak dystopian landscapes into a curious universe marked by damage and possibility."
—*Foreword*, starred review

"A treasure box, a mojo pot of stories to break your heart and mend it too. Nalo Hopkinson's fables, ghost tales, alien encounters, and automaton adventures are a sheer delight."
—Andrea Hairston, author of *Archangels of Funk*

"A powerful and salient reminder of just how amazing a storyteller we are graced with in the form of Nalo Hopkinson! This carefully curated collection is a tapestry of Nalo's mastery and truly displays what a master of the form can do."
—John Jennings, *New York Times* bestselling author and Hugo Award–winning comics creator

"It's with pleasure I can say this is another varied set with which [Hopkinson] shows a talent for making strange and thought-provoking tales with concerns including Western and Caribbean

cultures, gender, climate change, and adaptation and resilience."
—*Too Many Fantasy Books*

"*Jamaica Ginger* is a mélange of stories that spins together roots, dreams, and powerful tales the way only Nalo can. It's easy to get lost in the verses and images that drip from the page. A must-read."
—Tobias Buckell, author of *A Stranger in the Citadel*

"Hopkinson has gathered a collection of stories—a collection of worlds—that captivate."
—Kimberly Bain, writer and critic

"Each story in *Jamaica Ginger* surprises and delights. Nalo Hopkinson repeatedly draws on wild magic to examine human experiences so familiar that the tales feel like they're shaped from collective memories."
—Emily Pohl-Weary, author of *Not Your Ordinary Wolf Girl* and *How to Be Found*

Praise for Nalo Hopkinson

"A major talent."
—Karen Joy Fowler, author of *We Are All Completely Beside Ourselves*

"Nalo Hopkinson has had a remarkable impact on popular fiction. Her work continues to question the very genres she adopts,

transforming them from within through her fierce intelligence and her commitment to a radical vision that refuses easy consumption."
—*Globe and Mail*

"One of the best fantasy authors working today."
—*io9*

"An exciting new voice in our literature."
—*Edmonton Journal*

"Like Samuel R. Delany and Octavia E. Butler, [Hopkinson] forces us to consider how inequities of race, gender, class, and power might be played out in a dystopian future."
—*The News Magazine of Black America*

"Caribbean science fiction? Nalo Hopkinson is staking her claim as one of its most notable authors. . . ."
—*Caribbean Travel and Life*

"Hopkinson's prose is a distinct pleasure to read: richly sensual, with high-voltage erotic content and gorgeous details."
—SYFY.com

Also by Nalo Hopkinson

Novels
Brown Girl in the Ring (1998)
Midnight Robber (2000)
Under Glass (2001)
The Salt Roads (2003)
The New Moon's Arms (2007)
The Chaos (2012)
Sister Mine (2013)

Collections
Skin Folk (2001)
Report from Planet Midnight (2012)
Falling in Love with Hominids (2015)

Graphic Novels
The House of Whispers Vol. 1: The Power Divided (2018)
The House of Whispers Vol. 2: Ananse (2020)
The House of Whispers Vol. 3: Watching the Watchers (2020)

As Editor
Whispers from the Cotton Tree Root: Caribbean Fabulist Fiction (2000)
Mojo: Conjure Stories (2003)
So Long Been Dreaming (2004, with Uppinder Mehan)
Tesseracts Nine (2005, with Geoff Ryman)

JAMAICA GINGER
AND OTHER CONCOCTIONS

NALO HOPKINSON

TACHYON
SAN FRANCISCO

Tachyon Publications LLC
1459 18th Street #139
San Francisco, CA 94107
415.285.5615
www.tachyonpublications.com
tachyon@tachyonpublications.com

Series editor: Jacob Weisman
Project editor: Jaymee Goh

Print ISBN: 978-1-61696-426-9
Digital ISBN: 978-1-61696-427-6

Printed in the United States by Versa Press, Inc.
First Edition: 2024
9 8 7 6 5 4 3 2 1

Contents

Introduction

Nalo Hopkinson

READERS OFTEN ASK ME questions that presume I write with some kind of overarching plan. That I know what my themes, metaphors, and outcomes will be. There are writers who do write that way. Whereas my brain frequently resists linearity. I cobble together a messy first draft with scenes frequently written out of order and with no plan for them in mind. Then I figure out as much of that stuff as I can in subsequent revisions. I'm perpetually astounded that I'm able to complete anything at all.

My short stories are rarely published in the usual science-fiction and fantasy magazines. I do love those magazines. I'm not excluding myself from them deliberately (or at all, really). It's just that my fancy is often caught by unusual themes or projects in which I'm invited to participate. I don't write on spec any more (i.e., write pieces without a venue to which to submit them). I've never been the kind of writer who has a store of unpublished short stories that can be sent out at a moment's notice. Writing is hard! My ADHD/fibromyalgia/Non-Verbal Learning Disordered brain needs some kind of chemical jolt of excitement in order to be able to sustain it long enough to set words down. As a result of my publication habits, it may be difficult to track down my individually published short stories. So, I was tickled when Tachyon Publications offered for a second time to compile a collection of my stories published in the past few years. *Falling in Love with Hominids*, their previous collection of my short stories, is a favourite book of mine. (*Skin Folk*, my first short story collection, was published by Warner Aspect.)

When I was compiling *Falling in Love with Hominids* to send to the publisher, I—naturally, I thought—wrote a preface for each story, whether it was something about the genesis or context of the story, or some background fact that informed it, or just about what it was like writing it. I could have sworn I'd seen that done before. But it's possible I was thinking about multi-author fiction anthologies, since many people commented on how unique it was to see prefaces in a single-author collection. However, many readers seemed to especially appreciate the little prefaces. Perhaps because it gives some insight into some of the ways in which short stories can come into being? I don't know, but since readers found it useful the first time, here I am doing it again.

I'm also not sure what the prefaces have to tell anyone about where stories come from. I don't believe there's much generalization that can be usefully made about that. It's me trying to apply an inadequate amount of verbiage to how the process works *for me*. And it feels different each time. I'm now a professor of creative writing, teaching at the university level. But I've never been able to shake the feeling that I'm unable to capture for my students essential aspects of the creative process—at least, not in such a way that they can replicate it. What time of day do I write? Depends on my deadlines, my energy, and the whims of my brain chemistry. What type of music do I play in the background? Jesus Christ, none whatsoever! When there's music on, my mind literally can't retain anything but it. This is why I detest shopping in stores that pipe music in. I find myself standing in the aisles, turning in circles, trying to make my brain come up with even the name of the thing I came there to buy, while tinnitus bees buzz confusedly in my head (side effect of the fibromyalgia). I love music and dancing, but when I'm trying to concentrate on something else, music yanks my focus around on a short leash, and I feel increasingly disoriented and irritated by the inability to keep hold of the smallest idea until I get out of that environment. (Yes, yes, shopping lists. Sometimes, okay?)

What was I talking about? Oh, right; creative process and the questions people ask me about it. How do I do world-building? Fucked if I know. I've come up with an answer that sounds plausible, but is it really true? How do I know when a story is done? When its shape, arc, and trajectory have all brought the story to its end. There, does that help?

The process of writing a story, even a short one, feels bigger than I can express. Sometimes I can write a draft overnight. Sometimes it takes literally years. So, nowadays when I teach, I make a point of saying to students, "I'm going to try to teach to how to do this, but it's really difficult to explain fully. I wouldn't call anything I say a 'rule,' and I always feel as though I'm leaving something out. Maybe it's best to operate on the principle that anything I say about the craft of writing is a lie."

Oddly, they seem to understand that. I consider it an act of graciousness on their part.

So, here is a bunch of stories about people who are also

confounded about how their lives have brought them to the situation in which they find themselves.

Nalo Hopkinson
Vancouver, BC

P.S. My thanks to Nisi Shawl for the suggestion of the subtitle of this collection.

Quenching Our Story Thirst

Nisi Shawl

WHAT TRUTHS do you long to hear? What stories do you want to be told? You'll find at least one of them in this book.

Maybe more.

Start with the first story—there's a reason it's first. "And More Slow" depicts the half-visible, fully mysterious, face-to-face encounter the narrator has with what may very well be a fossilized alien embedded in the crust of Earth's moon. Through Hopkinson's description of this encounter, we gain our initial understanding of the author's essence: "A woman making of her very self a work of art and science."

Equipped with increased understanding, we can now venture onward to experience more encounters, more mysterious stories and strategies, peopled with players and workers and true pioneers, mothers and children and other offspring of Hopkinson's fertile imagination. Whether restricted in length or roomy, these stories are visions powered by fresh dreams, guided by the necessity of showing everyone how feelings are a form of intelligence it is far too dangerous for us to ignore.

So in "Child Moon," a mélange of folklore and cryptozoology, fierce love brings together a human mother and a nonhuman mother and shows them how to bridge the gap yawning between who their babies are *supposed* to be and who they've actually given birth to. In "Clap Back," rage and skepticism make performance art out of racist memorabilia. And in "Propagation," the author and we, her audience, join our hopes for a happy future to our traumatized pasts and our rebellious, activist, iconoclastic presents. With our collaboration, Hopkinson creates a brightly positive, *necessary* impossibility—a miraculous concatenation of scientific explorations, unscientific exceptions, and sheer, determined joy.

Chances are, a goodly portion of these stories are going to be new to you. As some are to me—but not all of them. I'd previously heard Hopkinson read "Child Moon" as part of the Clarion West Writing Workshop's instructor reading series; "Clap Back" first appeared in an anthology I coedited, swift substitution for an earlier version of "Broad Dutty Water," which I'd had to reject because of similarities to two other pieces already under contract. I originally read "Inselberg" in the wild, when it was republished in a 2021 issue of *Lightspeed Magazine.* It struck me then as an elegant way around the writerly problem of "Othering" nonstandard speech patterns: giving your narrative and your "dialect"-wielding characters the same voice. Rereading it now, preceded by Hopkinson's explanation of the puzzling-at-the-time title, I perceive so much more: the irony embedded in the tour guide's comic patter, the turnabout of dominant-culture members' loss of contextual clues, the simultaneous fun and seriousness of a situation in which rising seas swamp beaches, hotels, historical sites, and nuclear reactors—the last two representing both this island nation's contested past and the dubious future.

And of course I've read "Jamaica Ginger," this collection's title story before, because I'm its co-author.

There are two typical ways for writers to collaborate. One way makes each of them responsible for a certain part of their shared story: each is assigned a character, or a setting, or a time period, or some other element they're in charge of depicting. The other way is for the collaborators to hand the story back and forth between themselves, with or without the virtue of an outline—one either sketchy or well-fleshed-out—each of them adding a few paragraphs or pages on every turn they take. Hopkinson and I used the second method.

As she claims in her preface to that particular story, at the time Hopkinson was exhausted and at the end of her rope. However! When I became impatient with the length of time it was taking her to respond to my latest installment and wrote the rest of the story myself, she just laughed and rewrote it the way she wanted it to go.

The result is truly great. It is way, way better than the final pages I put together on my own. In fact, the entire story jumps and sings with liveliness it would never have had—*could* never have had—if it had relied on my ideas and words and choices and insights alone. And I'll warn you ahead of time not to try to read the finished story with the goal of figuring out who wrote which parts. I can't even tell that myself, although certain Hopkinsonian turns of phrase stick with me. For instance, I will never in my life forget her description of Plaquette's disgust with her mother's "stingy wisps of ham." Still, those shining peaks of literary artistry aside, the whole of "Jamaica Ginger" is exactly that: a whole.

Of the fifteen stories this book collects, I was already familiar with five. Perhaps some of you can top that number, but hey, this is not a competition. My point is that despite the fact that their original venues are as various as the genre stalwart *Magazine of Fantasy and Science Fiction* and limited-edition anthologies, that they range from cutting-edge digital publications through printed-on-paper mundane literary reviews, these are valuable works of art. Judging by the number I've managed to find and enjoy, you can tell that I've paid close attention to Hopkinson's writing career. Judging by how you're in actual possession of this book, you can tell that you do, too. Which is as it should be. Why?

Because of love, love and other bone-deep truths: realities surpassing mere facts. Because of the truths this author shares freely with you in her work. Because Hopkinson has the capacity to come up with exciting futures, hidden histories, and alternate versions of everything happening right here, right now. And because you and I can appreciate exactly what she's doing.

She brewed up these concoctions especially for us, which means our hearts and minds are the best places to keep them. They depict everything we want and more: beauty, strength, righteous fury, pleasure. Fears faced down. Hopes springing audaciously anew. Plots revealed, risks taken. These are the author's ingredients and here are her stories, all carefully prepared using ancient original recipes and freshly inspired ones.

Let's drink them in.

And More Slow

I find that increasingly, my work is being invited into spaces I didn't anticipate, such as comics, opera, visual art. "And More Slow" was written on the occasion of visual artist Rita McBride's exhibition at the Dia Art Foundation Gallery in New York. Rita, whose work is often informed and inspired by science fiction, commissioned me to curate an anthology of new science fiction to accompany the installation. The stories were written in response to the piece, which is called "Particulates," and Rita wanted me to include a story of my own. When I viewed her gigantic piece, I fancied that it could be an alien artifact. I liked the idea that it would be essentially undecipherable, unknowable, and that one of the few things we could learn was that it came from a female of its species. The anthology was also titled Particulates *and was self-published by the Dia. If you can, do get yourself a copy; there are wonderful stories in it you may not have read by the likes of Charlie Jane Anders and Victor LaValle. Rita's artwork was shown in the dark. It filled most of the*

*space. The installation included water dripping from
the ceiling and down the walls in places. I still remember the feeling of gravitas the installation imbued in
me—of awe and respect, the kind you might feel on
viewing the carcass of some massive, possibly intelligent
creature. Some of the authors came to the opening. We
did a group reading from the anthology right in the
gallery, by flashlight. It was a wonderful night, sharing
the different stories Rita's piece had inspired us to write.*

"THE THING IS," said Dr. Em, "we don't yet have a working
translation."

Saoirse nodded, then realized that she and Dr. Em couldn't
see each other in the dark. The chamber into which they'd
clambered seemed vast. It appeared to extend beyond the line
of vision. Difficult to tell. The light from the metres-long filaments glowed, but didn't illuminate very far. Dr. Em and her
team hadn't brought lights into the cave for fear of damaging or
degrading the data written in the bones.

Dr. Em continued, "We can peek in and perceive code. We
think we've even begun to identify repeating patterns. In a
way. With each new repeat, something changes."

"It cycles," Saoirse whispered.

"Never returns to the beginning, though. And there are
those in the community who still believe that what we've found
isn't an artificial language, but genetic material. There's a stone
ledge here where we can sit. Careful. It's damp in spots."

Saoirse sat. Gingerly, she reached a bare hand to touch the

cave wall behind her. Springy. Velveteen to the touch, and surprisingly dry. Moss?

She could half perceive Dr. Em taking a seat beside her. The chamber had a pleasant smell. Familiar. Saoirse couldn't quite put a name to it. The air was laden with liquid. It almost managed to contain the light that formed the creature's vast, slim bones—if creature it were, if bones—hollow and light as straws.

"We think she got stranded here. Migration, summer holiday; who knows what they were doing? She was a straggler. And if she exists, there must be others. Another intelligent race! Of course, they'll have died out long before the only organisms on Earth were unicellular."

Saoirse's eyes had adjusted to the dimness. She could see the glint on Dr. Em's teeth when she smiled. The doctor continued, "I shouldn't be fanciful when I'm in scientist mode, but I imagine her scurrying to catch up with the others."

"But failing," Saoirse said, "and dying, stuck in our cluster."

She ran her gaze, as she'd been doing since they entered, the length of the artifact. Sixteen filaments, evenly spaced in a circle, nipped in at the middle, opening out to the circle again. Like the bones of a djembe. Or a corset. That was all there was. "Why do you say 'she'?"

"It's one of two things we've figured out. The translation appears to be 'female of my species.'"

"She might not have been describing herself."

"True. But for now, in private with you, I call her 'she.'"

"The smell—" She recognized it now. It was the scent of rain falling on hot pavement.

"We're still analyzing its components."

"And she *made* our moon?"

"Perhaps, and not exactly. We think she was there when it was formed, give or take a few million years."

"Maybe she was on whatever wandering planet collided with proto-Earth so long ago to knock off debris that accumulated to form our moon."

"It's possible."

So many songs and poems, lunar inspired. Then humanity setting foot on it for the first time. "What's the second thing you figured out?"

"Another snippet. It appears to be 'Please tell my progenitors'—or perhaps it's 'my fathers'—and then an expression that could be the equivalent of 'the front door key's under the mat.'"

The sound of voices came from outside, official sounding, asking a question. Then the sound of footsteps coming their way. Saoirse said, "They've come to take her away from you, haven't they?"

Dr. Em inhaled quickly, sharply, like someone experiencing a blow to the body. "Yes. The minerals in her bones are very valuable. We can't even prove that this was a sentient creature. Some fools are still arguing that it's a natural formation, though unique. They're going to mine her away to nothing!"

Saoirse took the doctor's hand. It was warm to the touch. The lines and whorls of their palms and fingers met. "Not nothing," Saoirse said. "I know it's pallid comfort, but she was here, and she is here. She left her mark in her bones. In you and your team. In me. And she'll last forever in whatever widgets they're going to make of her."

Dr. Em stood and went closer to the filaments. "It's so beautiful, isn't it?"

"Yes." As some people came nearer—suits, clipboards—

Saoirse contemplated the gift of a woman making of her very self a work of art and science, fully taking up her space; all of it and more.

Can't Beat 'Em

As I said, I don't have folders of completed, unpublished stories. But I do have a folder of snippets, infrequently updated. Some of them are general story ideas. (Those tend to be the weakest. They feel programmatic, over-determined. I almost never use them.) Some are odd phrases or potential titles I thought or literally dreamed up. Some are random paragraphs that just came to me, unconnected to any story. In my years of writing, the random paragraphs have been the most useful. I'll take two or three of them, slam them together. If it works, the energy of creating a coherent story out of them is what generates the plot. Which type is "Can't Beat 'Em"? A little from Column Two and a little from Column Three. I lumped and layered them all together, working in my fascination with tardigrades and the climbing skills of ibexes, fuelling the whole with my frustration at there being not enough queer butch women as objects of desire in popular fiction.

"YEAH, THAT'S SOME CLOG," the plumber said. She pulled the metal-and-rubber snake out of the bathroom sink. Marisella wrinkled her nose at the gunk sticking to it. Whatever it had caught on in her drain had warped the metal and torn away bits of the rubber.

Marisella asked, "Can you fix it?" and, more softly, "Will it cost much?"

The plumber smiled at her. "Not a thing, hon. This one is Management's liability. They'll pick up the tab."

Well, that was a relief.

The plumber had a crinkly, friendly grin. And crisp short hair, and broad shoulders. Three of her knuckles were tattooed with the letters "T," "O," "Y." She was definitely Marisella's kind of girl.

Marisella sat on the lip of the bathtub to watch the plumber work. "I tried three bottles of that drain-clearing stuff, but no go."

The plumber shook her head. "That stuff doesn't work. Not on what's in there." She squatted down and reached into the tool kit at her feet. She pulled out a metal flask, unmarked. "What you wanna do, you see, is induce the new generation of sink throat monster that's growing too big for its comfy home in your drain there to motivate downwards and out into the larger sewer system; then to the river, and if it wants to go farther, to the ocean." She stood and unstoppered the flask. A fine thread of silver smoke lifted from it. "You can't kill these babies," she said, "but at least this one is still small enough you can encourage it to move along."

"What's your name?" Marisella asked, mesmerized by the flexing of the plumber's forearms as she opened the flask.

"Dot. Slide a few inches farther away, please, hon. Not that

I'm not enjoying your company, but the goop in here can dissolve flesh, and I would hate to splash any of it on you."

"Oh, of course." Marisella wondered how many teams Dot played for, and if any of them were hers.

Dot started carefully glugging the stuff in the flask down the drain. It was a viscous purple fluid. It smelled like dried shrimp, and it glowed.

Dot said, "Problem is, of course, that getting them out into the open sea only goes so far. Glups—that's what Management finally decided to call them—keep growing indefinitely. They're not sure how many of them are lining the ocean and river beds. Probably fewer than they think; it looks like the bigger ones eat the smaller ones."

That got Marisella's attention. "What?" She sidled past Dot's firm waist and luscious behind in its baggy work dungarees. She went and stood in the bathroom door.

"Yeah," said Dot. "We figure that's what preserves their immortality; eating a creature that doesn't die, but that can be eaten, digested, and incorporated into its host."

"You say Management sent you?"

"That's right, and you're lucky they called us when they did." She took a phial out of the toolbelt slung low around her belly. "When they get too big for the drains, these little devils can sometimes decide to come up instead of down. Wouldn't want a glup coming at you while you're sound asleep in your cozy little bed."

"It's a king," Marisella told her absent-mindedly. There was something grainy inside the phial, like ground black pepper. "What happens if they come up instead of going down?"

Dot peered at the grains and gave Marisella a reassuring smile. "Well, you're never going to find out, are you? I got you."

She uncorked the phial and poured the grains in after the purple goo. She continued, "Our planet's waters are drying up. Glups drinking it all. That's what the politicos like to say. Truth is, we aren't helping, what with our having created global warming and all. We're just making the cycle go faster. Whoops!"

Marisella yelped. A slim black thread was wriggling out of the drain. It slapped against the inside of the sink basin and started questing around blindly. It reached for Dot's wrist. Dot shook it off. She bent and pulled something out of her tackle box that looked like the offspring of a plunger and a bottle of holy water. By then, five more fighting threads had wormed their way out of the drain.

Dot said, "All right then, baby. You wouldn't go down, so I guess it's out for you." She enjoined battle. It seemed to involve alternately squirting and plunging with the mystery tool. In between, she huffed at Marisella, "Because it is a cycle, you know? Took Management long enough to figure out that when a planet has been totally consumed by glups until all that's left is a planet-sized knot of them, their collective heat ignites them. They become a sun. Ah, you little devil, you! Anyway, those particular suns eat other stars. The digested star stuff is pushed to the bottom of the singularity well, where it generates more planets. And so the cycle continues. There's something in there about the heat death of the universe. Maybe that's where it all ends. But maybe it's just the largest glup of all swallowing everything and shitting out new beginnings."

She'd beaten back all but one of the threads. She yanked with her gloved hands at that one. Slowly, she began pulling whatever was at the end of it out of the drain.

"Don't worry about splashing. The black stuff neutralizes the purple stuff."

"You're sure?"

"Yeah. Done this a million times. Well, three times, anyway. Management thinks it's having some success with a project of breeding new forms of tardigrades. Those things are so tiny! Don't let that fool you, though; they can survive boiling, freezing, and vacuum. We've found them on comets arcing in from deepest space."

"We?"

"Maybe that's where they came from in the first place. Maybe tardigrades can kill our glups for us. Though I'm not sure it makes sense to kill them."

Marisella nodded. "Glups are the engine of the universe."

Dot laughed, joyous and belly-deep. "Exactly. You understand me."

With a pop and a triumphant, "Ha!" from Dot, the thing from Marisella's drain came free. "Here we go; okay if I dump it into this toothbrush mug?"

"Um, yeah."

The glup had curled a thread around Dot's finger. Marisella had to help her snip the thread. The monster fell wetly into her blue ceramic toothbrush mug. She and Dot contemplated it. It pulsed once, making the mug quiver as though it'd been filled with mercury. Dot said, "It barely looks alive, doesn't it? Don't worry; the purple stuff will keep it pacified."

With two fingers, she peeled the curl of black thread from her glove, popped it into her mouth, and swallowed. Marisella felt her own throat working in response. "What're you going to do with it?" she asked Dot.

"Ocean. It's only forty-five minutes to the beach. Maybe one of its bigger cousins will take care of it for us. Or vice versa."

"I can take it there," Marisella blurted.

"You're sure? You'd have to do it within a day or two, before the suppressant wears off."

"I'm sure." She wasn't. She just knew she didn't want to let the glup go right away. Marisella's head was swimming. She thanked Dot, offered her some cold water. "It's filtered," she said. "And it's from the fridge."

Dot slugged back a glass of that, no ice. She and Marisella exchanged numbers. "So you can call me," Dot told her. "You know, in case you need anything." Marisella just nodded and escorted her out. She'd probably call Dot sooner or later. She just had too much on her mind right now.

Marisella went back into the bathroom. The baby glup lay curled on itself in her toothbrush mug, exhausted.

Such a simple shape it had. Slimy greenish-black, shiny and uncomfortably, organically slug shaped. It had gone all bumpy and dull, and it seemed to be humming; vague notes almost too low for Marisella to hear. A small, sad eye materialized out of the mass of it and stared glumly at Marisella.

Marisella didn't care if she were part of a greater plan. Life was too good. There were hot butch plumbers around, and so many new things to try. She didn't want to die, not ever.

Dot said that whatever consumed an immortal glup became immortal.

She took a deep breath and picked up the mug. It was heavier than she expected.

Raw, or stir-fried with some nice onions, maybe in a cream sauce? Maybe invite Dot to dinner?

She took the glup to the kitchen.

Child Moon

I was in the middle of a long nighttime flight back from some event in which I'd participated, I don't even remember what. I may have been the headliner. I take Dramamine in order to fly; otherwise I experience motion sickness. The Dramamine works, but leaves me in a hypnagogic state where I drop into and out of consciousness and dream/hallucination. In that condition during that particular flight, I opened my eyes to see that we were drifting by the light of a full moon across a deep, deep valley surrounded by high mountains. It should have been vomit inducing, but it was also fucking beautiful. I tucked it away to use later, and drifted back into half-sleep. At some point in time, perhaps even on that flight, I briefly drifted from semi to full consciousness with the phrase "the girls between the rivers" in my head and was able to remain awake long enough to write it down. When Jo Walton contacted me a few months into the pandemic and asked me to contribute a short story to a fundraiser anthology, I knew I wanted to put that scene and that phrase into it. The anthology was in the spirit of Boccaccio's 1353 book The Decameron, *a collection of linked short stories in which a group of people living during the great plague called the "Black Death" are hiding from Death in a secluded villa and telling each other stories to pass the time—in other words, sheltering in place, hoping death wouldn't find them, just as the modern-day world was doing in the face of another plague. The anthology concept really caught my fancy. The story was written in days. It be's that way sometimes.*

Spoiler here: I gave a public reading of that story a little while later (via Zoom, in the brave new world we've made). Someone in the audience asked me whether the human child in the story survived. I had to ask her which one of them she meant. In any case, I didn't know the answer. The story ended where it ended.

I'll always be impressed by and grateful toward the sign language interpreter who did a live interpretation of the story as I read it. She took a piece set in no world that has ever existed and imbued it, near as I could tell, with the full sensorium and emotional landscape I'd attempted to convey in written words.

A NOISE WAKES AMY. She sits up on the sleeping pallet she shares with her husband, Dorin, in their one-room cottage. The baby is in its basket, an arm's length away. It is chuckling to itself. It is holding its blanket between tiny hands and ripping it to shreds with small, sharp teeth. That's what had woken

Amy up: the soft chortle; the sound of cloth tearing. Beside Amy, Dorin sleeps, oblivious.

The baby's been getting worse. Amy has promised Dorin to stop her monthly moondark pilgrimages to the spring. He offered to accompany her, but the woodwife says it must be the mother alone.

Dorin doesn't believe in the woodwife's cures, and doesn't want Amy going out in the cool of night. Besides, he says, there might be leopards up there in the mountains.

But maybe just one last time. Maybe it will work this time.

She has to take the baby with her; it's due another feeding soon. If Amy isn't there to give the baby suck, its hungry keening will awaken Dorin, and he will see that Amy isn't in the cottage. He will worry. Then he will have to feed the baby himself, and he's already so tired!

Amy rises quietly. She wraps the baby in its shredded blanket, and then cocoons it in one of her shawls, for warmth. Holding her bundled child to her bosom, Amy tiptoes out of the cottage. She has to latch the door from the outside, since it has no lock. But she'll be back before sunrise opens Dorin's eyes. They keep a pail and spear just outside the cottage door. Clutching the handle of the pail and the middle of the spear in one hand, Amy takes the path toward the mountains.

The girls between the rivers don't come down to the valleys. Amy has heard them warbling to each other from hill to hill during her climbs up to the source of the River Elta to fetch a bowl of water to wash her baby's hair.

This is Amy's third visit up to the spring. She made the first pilgrimage in the month the baby was born sickly, and one the next month, because the baby wasn't better. The woodwife

says it must be water collected on nights when there's no light
shining on it from the mad-making moon.

*The rivers Elta, Eisel, Ginife and Lucasta run between the
mountains like the fingers of a hand a child presses into wet sand
on a beach. The mounded sand between the fingers are the Grief
Mountains, called by some the Goat Mountains. But really, there
are no goats, though perhaps there were at some point. Perhaps the
girls ate them.*

Once she's well on her way up the mountain and she can
see the shadow of the sleeping village below her, Amy pauses to
pull back a corner of the baby's swaddling.

The child is awake and calmly alert. Amy hasn't seen it sleep
in the two months of its life; not once. It lies quietly in its basket
all night, eyes open and looking around. Its eyes are growing
bigger. It has taken to biting Amy's breast when she gives it
suck. No two-month-old baby should have teeth.

Her baby is beautiful; chubby, with a head full of fat curls
of hair, and those big, bright eyes in its brown face; those tiny,
milk-coloured teeth, like kernels of young corn. Even Dorin
agrees that it's beautiful, though he's doubtful about its pointed
teeth and white hair; markers, along with its eyes and its velvety
skin, of its illness. The rest of the village has been muttering
and staying away. Such children aren't born often, and don't
usually live this long.

Amy doesn't care. Whenever she gives suck to her baby—
milk with droplets of blood in it from the baby's overeager
teeth—a feeling of serenity comes over her, and she knows all
is well. She thinks it's the baby doing that somehow, but she
doesn't mind. She just wants to make her child normal and
healthy so it will live.

Amy folds the swaddling snugly around the child again. She

clutches it closer against her aching bosom and resumes her climb. She's about halfway up the mountainside. Tonight, snow frosts the tips of the short, sparse mountain grasses. They crunch underfoot. It's been winter in the high, high mountains for a month. The pail hangs by its handle from Amy's wrist, the one beneath the baby's rump. With every step, the pail knocks against the strings of wife beads around Amy's waist, under her wrapper. Amy hopes the clacking noise will scare away any leopards.

Is that a sly rustling in the low, twisted mountain acacias beside the path? Amy stills her feet for an impossibly long handful of heartbeats, listening. Nothing. She starts walking again, a little faster.

Rustle.

Amy stops.

Silence.

She tells herself the sound is her, when she walks and the hem of her wrapper scrapes against the frost-rimed grass. She keeps climbing the mountain path, in a darkness so black it has a nap, like the dense fur of the village's barkless dogs.

Amy has gotten to know the way pretty well, but she still thanks Bondyè for the faint glow of frost edging everything.

The girls between the rivers feed on the moon. They sip from Her light night by night. Night by night, they bleed Her. They grow fat and torpid as ticks on a dog. The moon withers away till it dies. The girls between the rivers grow lean and hungry, their eyes avid, their ears keen. They huddle whimpering in their caves in the mountains, praying for the night sky to bless them again. If their prayers are heard, the child moon rises from the moon's ashes a week later. The cycle begins again.

From inside the twisted forest comes a dopplering yelp,

suddenly cut off. Amy gasps and swings towards the noise. The
baby, too, half-turns towards the sound. It's cooing, its eyes
wide and bright. Its movement sets the pail a-swing, knock-
ing the spear out of Amy's grasp. The bulk of the baby in her
arms prevents her from seeing where it landed. The rustling
through the forest and the panic-footed thud of something
fleeing is coming closer. She needs the spear! Amy stoops with
her baby—the pail, its handle still trapped around her wrist,
clacks painfully against her knees—and blindly scrabbles for
the spear in the short, spiky brush.

Her sudden crouch is what saves them.

A creature bursts out of the forest, bleating. Amy and her
baby are directly in its path. Amy has a fleeting impression of
four spindly legs. Long, whitish fur. The creature lurches in
surprise at the apparition that is Amy and her baby. It's moving
too quickly to detour around them. It barely manages to twist
its headlong momentum into a clumsy leap. Amy has her baby
on the ground beneath her. She curls her body protectively over
it. The claws of one of the creature's back legs score Amy's
shoulder, and then it leaps clear of them. It dashes across the
path and enters the forest on the other side. Amy's searching
hand closes around the shaft of her spear. She is still on her
knees when she hears something else coming through the
brush. Then it is upon them; a brindled shadow, as wide across
as the heavy double wooden doors of the house of worship in
the village. Intent on hunting the first creature, it doesn't seem
to notice Amy and baby. It will brush by them, barely. Parental
fierceness and something else half-realized put steel in Amy's
thews. Still on one knee over her child, Amy braces the butt
end of the spear against the ground. Two-handed, she pulls
the tip up to shoulder height. The beast thunders by, so close

that Amy can smell the must of its fur. The spear connects, jarring Amy's arms. The beast's momentum nearly drags the spear from her hand, but she holds on. The creature snarls and briefly twists away from the head of the spear. But it keeps galloping forward in the direction of its prey, until it, too, disappears into the scrub forest on the other side of the path.

Amy sits down hard. She's breathing heavily, tearily. Her whole body is shuddering with reaction. She manages to lift her child, peel back its swaddling. The baby is unharmed. Its eyes are wide and fascinated. They reflect the faint glow of the frost-rimmed grass.

The baby slobbers at Amy's fingers, which are wet with the beast's blood. The child is hungry. Amy lets it lick the blood from her fingers awhile as she catches her breath a little. Then she pulls down one side of her tunic and puts the baby to her breast. She winces as it bites and latches. It sucks contentedly at her mingled milk and blood. It clutches one of her fingers in its small, trusting fist. Its tiny cheeks work in and out. Amy kisses the top of the baby's head, the tender spot at its crown that smells faintly of sweetlime blossoms. The times when Amy has been too weak and blood-let to give suck to their unweaned child, Dorin has in desperation put the baby to his own breast; let it bite him there; let it suckle his blood. He doesn't mind, he says. This is his child, too.

Now that the disturbance has passed, the small night animals in the knurled forest commence their wheeting and peeping noises once more. Amy knows she must get going again. She could nurse her baby while walking, but she's drained. Just a bit more rest. Her shoulder stings where the first creature's hoof grazed it. Her head is spinning. So she sits, breathing herself calm.

There are spots of the beast's blood on the path. And it comes to Amy what she glimpsed out of the corner of her eye as the first creature fled. Why she went to its defense.

After it leapt over her and her baby, it landed on two spindly, goatish legs. It kept running that way, upright, like a person. And clinging to the fur of its back was a small, naked child.

The memory galvanizes Amy into a crouch, but she needs to hold onto her upright spear in order to lever herself up the rest of the way. The baby seems a lot heavier. Amy doggedly continues on up the path. Her head is swimming. She is panting. Her shoulder throbs, though her arms feel numb. The numbness creeps over her torso. She can't even tell whether the baby is still nibbling at her breast. Her thoughts are asking her whether she shouldn't perhaps go back down the mountain for help? But her sensible mind is far away, no louder than a tickle in her skull. She has to get to the spring. That's why she came up here. She can remember that. Back is complicated. Continuing forward is simple.

There is a tree up ahead, just at the edge of the path. Its trunk is perhaps the thickness of her calf, but that's strong enough. Amy takes one wobbly step after another and all but falls against the tree. Her spear falls from nerveless fingers. Is she even holding the baby anymore? She tries to squeeze it more tightly against her chest. It cries, but she cannot, will not let it fall.

Two small, sharp hands grab her by her upper arms. A pair of huge eyes, their depths glowing, looks into hers. The face is slim, foxlike, hairless, but surrounded by long, whitish fur. Amy screams. The face snarls, showing pointed teeth. As Amy's legs give way and she falls, she hears the chuckling of her child.

The sound of trickling awakens her. There is water, only

a few steps from her face, plinking downward tunefully over rocks, to disappear underground a little farther off. It is the spring that leaps down the mountainside to feed the River Elta. Amy is lying on the chilly ground at the third highest point of the Grief Mountains.

She sits up. Her pail and spear lie nearby. Her head is clearer. The feeling has returned to her arms, though her fingers still tingle a little. The wound on her shoulder stings much less than before. Amy pats it, and something flattish, dark and damp sloughs off onto the ground. She picks it up. It appears to be a poultice, but she doesn't recognize the smell of the herbs of which it is made.

The vista out over the valleys takes Amy's breath away with its beauty. Light limns the edges of the mountains. Darkness pools in the vast spaces between. The air is so deep between sky and valley, it's like another country. A country of air. Her village is somewhere down there. Amy sees she had been wrong; tonight is not the last night of moondark, but the first night of the child moon. It hangs in the night sky, a crescented sliver of silver, throwing a bluish glow over the scene. Maybe any water she draws tonight won't help her baby after all.

Her baby! The back of Amy's throat springs water, as though she's going to vomit: part terror that the baby is nowhere in sight; part shame because it wasn't the first thing she thought of when she returned to consciousness. Heartsick, she checks the spring first. She's terrified of what she might find. But if the baby has fallen or crawled into the water, she can't see it. For panicked heartbeats, Amy wheels and wheels about on the plateau, not knowing what to do.

She stills herself. Stifles her sobs. She must think. But then she remembers the wide, heavy beast, hunting deadly in the darkness, and fear for her child rises up so strongly in her that she chokes on it. She grabs up her spear and starts running, stumbling in the darkness. She tracks back and forth from the stream and away, working her way downward.

Nothing. Nothing.

Someone is coming up the path. Amy has a brief, mad hope that it is Dorin, somehow come to her rescue.

The apparition is not Dorin. It is pale against the dark forest. It walks on two legs, dragging something heavy behind it. It is slightly shorter than she. And it is clutching her baby.

Amy runs towards, it, yelling and brandishing her spear. She shouts to the creature to leave her child alone. But it doesn't appear frightened. It lets go the thing it is dragging. It stands and waits for her, dandling the baby. Amy bares her teeth. She's ready to bite and slash and rend with them if she must, to protect her child.

When Amy is close enough, she snatches the baby away. The baby gives a startled wail. Amy inspects it frantically—has the creature hurt it?

It's not her child crying. The sound is coming from behind the creature's head. The creature reaches up and back with small, sharp-fingered hands. It swings something over its head and into its arms. It coos comfortingly at the bundle it holds. Its own baby. The creature tenderly licks the baby's tears away, then gives the baby suck on one of its own nipples. It is the same creature that leapt over Amy farther down the mountain.

The creature keeps a wary eye on Amy. It—she—stoops and resumes dragging something large and brindled along behind her; the beast that Amy jabbed with her spear. It is very dead. Amy can see her spear gash in its side, red and working, like a mouth. The goat-legged woman is dragging the beast by one foot. After a moment's hesitation, Amy catches up. She tosses her spear down onto the beast's shaggy belly. She takes one of the beast's other legs and helps with the pulling. Each paw is the size of Amy's head. She can't hold the whole paw. She has to twist her fist in its fur instead. Stretched out, the thing is nearly as long as Amy and the other woman laid end to end. Its fur swallows light. Two pairs of tusks cross its upper and lower jaws. Its head has been nearly decapitated. The long-eared head bounces on the ground as they go. A dribble of blood trails from its neck. It wasn't Amy who made that killing blow. The beast is *heavy*, yet the goat-legged woman pulls it easily. She doesn't need Amy's help.

As they clamber up the path, Amy sneaks glances at the other woman. Her face, hands, and feet, like Amy's, are brown and hairless. Her narrow face with its merest suggestion of a muzzle is quite well-favoured. Amy tries to speak with her, to ask her who or what she is. The woman makes chuffing sounds, but Amy does not understand.

They lay the beast down beside the spring. The woman checks Amy's wounded shoulder, muttering her coughing speech the while. It could be an apology. The woman kneels and picks some leaves from beside the spring. She chews them, pats them into another poultice, and places it on Amy's shoulder. As the poultice draws out the remainder of the poison that came from the woman's claws, she hands Amy back her spear and with one stroke of her clawed fingers, lays the beast open from craw to cradle-string. Amy begins to wonder who had been hunting whom back there when she and her child got in the way of the chase.

The woman slices out organs, lays them aside. She removes a slab of liver that she rinses in the spring, then tears into rough strips with her claws. She offers one of the strips to Amy's baby. Amy says, "It's too young for meat."

But the baby takes the offal with eager paws and starts gnawing messily at it. The woman gives her own child a piece of the liver. It gums it, then tosses it onto the ground and goes back to suckling.

Amy unwraps her shawl from her baby. She spreads the shawl out onto the ground. The two women lay their children down upon it. They sit awkwardly side by side, two shunned mothers soaking their feet in the cool spring water. Amy eats a piece of the liver when offered. It is both fatty and stringy, deliciously unctuous. The babies roll and crawl around, warbling and chuckling at each other. The night is peaceful again.

Eventually, the child moon begins dipping into the valley. The sky is lightening from black to deep blue. It is time to go home. Amy stands. She swings the goat woman's baby into her arms to give it to its mother. Her new friend picks up Amy's baby. The two women stand there, each holding the other's child. Amy's baby is red-muzzled, red-handed. A string of raw liver dribbles from the corner of its mouth. The goat woman's baby has muddy hands. Stubby, blunt fingers. A muddy face. No teeth yet. It has already fallen asleep on Amy's shoulder.

Her own child never sleeps.

The women's eyes meet. A decision is jointly made.

The goat woman accompanies Amy some distance down the mountain, to the point where the brindled beast attacked. Then she nuzzles and sniffs her child's neck, licks some mud off its forehead. The child's head lolls a little on Amy's shoulder. It doesn't wake as its first mother says goodbye. Amy touches her baby's arm. For not quite the last time, she strokes the near-invisible down that covers her child's skin; not unusual for a baby to be born with lanugo, but it should have fallen off long since. Amy now understands that the down will remain, will grow long, as will its fingers and toes. That the mild drunkenness that comes from the baby's bite will mature, with age, into a powerful soporific it will be able to deliver with a single swipe of its hind claws.

The goat woman chuffs at Amy, then heads into the forest. Amy continues down the hill. She will tell everyone that her baby was miraculously cured by the spring water. Everyone except Dorin; him, she will tell the truth. He will grieve, but she will make him understand. She will take him up the mountain with her sometimes on the first night of the child moon, so the two children can play together. Until her child is old enough to speak, that is; old enough to have memory. They will stop going up the mountain then. She will not put the burden on a child to keep so profound a secret. By then, he'll have playmates amongst the children of the village. He'll forget his eldritch friend soon enough.

Covenant

I was approached by artist Liam Young, who was working on a big multimedia project called "Planet City." As part of the project, he had solicited writers to create science fiction stories based on the premise that in order to preserve Earth, its human population had retreated into a single city, leaving the rest of the planet undisturbed until its ecologies stabilized from the damage we're currently doing to them. It turns out it's theoretically possible. My mind tends to be contrary, though. Liam wanted a science fiction story, but what I came up with was a fable.

PROVERB: Your child wants to forget it was the baby whose ass you used to wipe.

Understand, this City of Covenant wasn't always the City. Wasn't always the place where all Earth's humans lived. For millennia before Covenant came to be, people had infested the whole of the

Earth, devouring her goodness and shitting out ingratitude and poison into the air, the soil, and the water. But then Earth began to defend Herself. She spit our poison back at us in the form of plagues and conflagrations. Damned near killed us all. So we had to learn manners, y'feel me? Had to learn to respect the Lady, to stop chomping on her like a teething baby that still wants the titty. We had to let Her have Herself back, to heal. So we built the City of Covenant and retreated into it. We vowed to take nothing more from Mama Earth than we had already. We vowed to discard nothing more. We vowed ever after to break stuff we wasn't using down into its component parts and remake it into stuff we needed, over and again, world without end.

Thing is, we been living here in Covenant so long that we kinda forget the way of it happening, so we make up stories about it.

Naw, that ain't true. Course we remember. Ain't we still designing and moulding the modest magnificence that is the Ark of the Covenant? Don't we have history books and textbooks, and more being written all the time? Don't we have scientists and teachers and artists and griots that carry our histories for us in one form or another and won't let us disremember them? We ain't forget shit. The real truth of it is, human beings make up fancy stories to tell each other. It is the most particular thing about us as animals.

This is the story as they told it once when I was visiting my sweets in Arrondissement 21,000, in the tall purple tower called Tampopo. Night times, after the sun's gone down and is no longer throwing sparkling traceries of sunshine through the hollow, mirrored webs that pierce all the towers in multiple places, bringing life-giving light down into the City's depths, folks who want to hang and jaw with other folks, who'd rather be doing that than going to the movies or fucking or going dancing or who knows what all? I mean, they might do some of those things tomorrow or next week, or in an hour or two. But for now, those folks want to go out onto the layered collars of balconies that ring Tampopo from top to bottom. They want to suck on a birra or a doob, watch their pickens climbing from level to level, and yell at them to take care. And they want to share stories, lobbing them from one balcony to another, each balcony continuing a piece of the tale. It's a bearing of witness, a sharing. And so what if they're bearing witness to something that's made the fuck up? Fact is, there's a deep truth in there, strong and curved as a spine.

Here's what they shared that night:

It began out in the World laid waste. It began with a potato. The eye of a potato, to be precise. This woman named Alillia, she had cut out the eyes of last night's potatoes for dinner with a sharp, sharp knife. She tossed the peel and the eyes into the garbage, 'cause in those days, you tossed away shit you could use. It was legal, and folks even thought it was necessary. Don't get me started.

But one eye had escaped Alillia. She found it on the kitchen table next morning, a little stubby pale thing lying there like a maggot, ready to dry up and die.

She picked the potato eye up and was about to throw it away, same as she'd done with the rest.

The single, accusing bud stared up at her.

On her kitchen table was an empty waxed paper cup. Her morning coffee had been in there when she got it from the shop on the way back from her morning walk. Yes, paper covered in wax to make it waterproof. And then they'd *throw it away,* y'feel me? Any road, Alillia's steel cooking spoon held up when she used it to dig some soil out of the grass verge beside the sidewalk of her building. She had to do it that way. She wasn't allowed a garden where she lived, wasn't allowed a patch of soil. All the ground in her wee city was covered with paving, or buildings, or something called "lawn grass" that needed watering and watering, but that wasn't good for nothing, not to eat, not to improve the soil, not even really for pretty, to hear the old folks who were alive back then tell it. Them folks who lived out on the World was crazy.

So yeah, our Alillia. She filled the cup with soil, buried the potato eye in it. The dryness of the soil against her fingers made her throat feel parched. Maybe the eye felt parched, she wondered? She didn't know shit about growing stuff, but she'd seen some things on TV. She ran some water from the kitchen tap into the cup. Then she put the cup onto the windowsill and forgot about it.

Until the evening she came home from her job—that's a place they had to go most days back then to do stuff they didn't like all freakin' day and somebody paid them a lil' bit o' money for it (money's a whole 'nother crazy story; I'll tell you 'bout that another time)—and that Alillia, she looked into the cup on her kitchen windowsill and discovered an inch of eyestalk with two green leaves peeking out above the soil, complete with eye. At first she thought her own eyes were deceiving her, until the eyestalk blinked. She touched it with a gentle fingertip. The eye part of the stalk retreated, snail-like, into itself, then emerged again. The iris was yellow-green. It shimmered.

The soil in the cup was nearly dried out. Alillia poured a little water into it. The eye watched her warily. She put the cup back onto the windowsill, then scurried to her fridge to see what else was in the crisper.

In just a few weeks, she had a little parade of coffee cups on the windowsill. Another potato eye. A kohlrabi top that was now growing two small paws, or maybe they were hands. A watermelon seed had sprouted a green lump that appeared to have two nipples; the root part of a green onion had yielded a snaky, scaled green tail that wagged slowly. Two pink, fleshy frills came from a chunk of horseradish. They seemed to prefer being kept wet. The squash seeds never grew at all, but the pineapple crown was apparently turning into many small jaws with green, serrated baby teeth.

When her indoor jungle seemed sturdy enough, Alillia transplanted them all into whatever she could find; empty coffee cans, a bucket with a hole in the bottom (good for drainage, right?), rusted pots. She arranged them all along the outside wall of her ground-floor apartment. The assemblage became the talk of her small apartment complex. In a few weeks, she knew more of her neighbours by name than she ever had before. Yup, people didn't talk to each other much back then, 'less they really wanted to. People had enough space to ignore each other. That part wasn't so bad. Anyroad, Philomene and Taisha in 212 suggested soft strips of T-shirt material for attaching the ever-lengthening eyestalks to the sticks Alillia had stuck into the containers to support the plants. Vayu in 302 and his two daughters, Stevie and Joan, helped her to keep the plants watered. One Sunday afternoon, the guy who lived in 111 wheeled over to where Alillia was gently cleaning the teeth in the pineapple jaws with a soft toothbrush. On his lap was a garbage bag full of coffee grounds. He said they'd make good mulch. He'd even dried them out in his oven for her. "But they're cool now," he said. So you see, them people back then weren't entirely stupid or wasteful. They were our ancestors, after all. Must have been some good in them, as there is in us.

The guy's name was Eladon, and he wondered if Alillia might like to go see a movie with him some day. Alillia's heart thumped as they made it a date. She'd noticed his strong arms. Now she'd finally get to ask him what the tattoos on them were. (No, Zetta, I don't know what they were. They can be whatever you want them to be.)

Folding chairs and picnic umbrellas began to appear in the courtyard, surprising as gills on a horseradish. All summer, the neighbours hung out there, chatting, sharing food and beer, watching their children romp, like we're doing right now. The plants grew big enough to warp and burst their pots, as the apartment complex waited to see what rough beast would assemble itself from Alillia's efforts.

Nobody saw it happen. Just one morning Alillia came out of her unit and found all the plants had vacated their containers. And what's more, they weren't plants no more. Instead, lying on the ground was a tiny green dragon, no bigger than a basset hound. No wings; it was a Laidly Worm. It just crawled where it wanted to go. But it didn't go anywhere much. It knew it had a good thing right where it was. It ate a lot, and it grew fast. What it liked to eat best was the stuff people in the apartment complex threw away—the tasty, yeasty vegetable peelings and bits of rotting prote, and by prote I mean actual chopped-up animals someone had grown and killed for them, not the animal product we grow in vats nowadays. Them folks, they killed beings like themselves and ate them! I know, right? Bugfuck crazy, and mean into the bargain.

The dragon grew, and began eating other discarded things: old, sprung sofas and torn clothes and broken-down bookcases.

It grew so big that it couldn't crawl any more. It settled itself around the apartment complex. Folks had to clamber over it to get to their jobs. But they didn't mind, 'cause no other apartment complex had a cool pet dragon.

When the dragon grew big enough, it started eating other crazy things that people out in the World plagued Her with in those days: sidewalks, and cars, and lawn grass. It got so huge that it covered the apartment complex that had birthed it. Then it got so big that it covered the whole neighbourhood, and then the whole wee city. It shat out mounds of rich, organic stuff. It shat out towers of the stuff. And the people in the city hollowed out the towers, and made homes in them. And they didn't have to go to their jobs no more, because they had everything they needed right there. They could work at whatever they pleased, and have time to hang with their friends and their pickens and their sweets.

And that's how the City of Covenant began, so some say. What's more, they say that one day, if we honour our covenant with the Earth and show Her that we're grown enough to act grown, She'll send us another baby dragon to feed and care for as it grows and grows. Only this one will have wings. And one day it'll be big and strong enough, and it'll unfurl the green translucent glory of those wings. They'll be so huge, those wings, that they'll be able to sail on the wind of the sun's light. That dragon will sail us on its broad back and take us to find other beautiful worlds. Not to use up, mind, but to live in and cherish.

Wire bend, story end.

Ally

This story doesn't sit easily with me. It was written to submit to an anthology of ghost stories. (The editor declined it.) And what you have here is a piece of short fiction with a trans woman protagonist, written by a cis woman. The basic plot is disquieting and eerie, as ghost stories are. But in addition, to my ear, it doesn't convince as something written from or addressed to an insider perspective. It feels like what it is: a cis woman speaking to other cis people—because we need to stand up, too. It's my attempt to be supportive to my trans and gender nonbinary friends, colleagues, lovers, acquaintances, fellow humans in my communities, as there are, always have been, and always will be such people in communities all around the world. Learning to speak out against violence from a place of privilege is an awkward, uncomfortable process. I wouldn't call this story adroit. But as Canadian poet Nourbese has said, "She tries her tongue, her silence softly breaks."

It'd been a warm, sunny spring afternoon. The grass in the cemetery was green, the roses and lavender in the wreaths fragrant. Iqbal's funeral had been a quiet affair, all things considered.

Our circle was getting too old for the type of soap opera drama that had marked our younger years. We'd lived for enough decades that my friends and I had settled into some kind of rhythm, had dared to allow some of our sharp edges to be burnished smooth.

So by the time of Iqbal's funeral, Joachim had long since given up staging drunken screaming matches in parking lots with Jésus for stealing Joachim's boyfriend Steve, lo these many years ago. After all, soon after Steve had left him, Joachim had met and bottomed to Randall at a play party, and they'd been together ever since. Randall had ceased lamenting the flawless beauty of his youth to anyone who would (or wouldn't) listen. He'd started dating a couple of eager smooth-skinned houseboys, vetted by Joachim. The young men kept Joachim's and Randall's boots spit-polished. Randall had let his hair grow in grey, waxed his mustachios, and relaxed into his daddy role.

Munroe had become an actual daddy as a result of a drunken evening with his dyke friend Alice. He ended up sharing custody of the little girl with her—mostly amicably, with some glaring exceptions. "Baby" Tina was twenty-two years old now. She'd attended the service with hugs for all her uncles and me, her aunty. Almost everyone had remembered to call me Sally. After all, it'd been seven years. Pete did slip up and call me "Jack . . . er, Sal," but I didn't bite his head off; he was, after all, burying his husband. But it's been seven fucking years, dude, and you're still making that mistake?

When I transitioned, Pete's awkwardness about it had cooled

our friendship down quite a bit. So as I stood beside the grave site with the others, watching the coffin being lowered mechanically into the hole and longing to get out of the black pumps that were crushing my toes in two very stylish vices, I was surprised when my phone buzzed with a text from Pete: *The bar in an hour? Just you and me?*

Well. It'd been years since he and I had hung out like that, but I knew exactly which bar he meant. I texted back, *Make it an hour and a half.* To underline that I wasn't going to let him "Jack" me again, I added, *Momma needs to slip into something more comfortable.*

I only stopped at home long enough to switch my heels for flats and give the hubby a squeeze, but Pete was already waiting when I got to the bar. He was nursing a virgin Manhattan, extra maraschino cherries. Nowadays, sugar was his drug of choice. He looked glumly up at me and kicked out the chair opposite his. The haunted look in his eyes made my heart ache. I sat. He said, "Rye and soda?" I didn't even need to nod. He knew what I liked, and was already signaling the waitress.

Two women sitting together at the bar gave me the side-eye. They leaned their heads together to talk, scowling at me the whole time. Easy to figure what they had their panties in a twist about. "You okay?" I asked Pete. "Never mind. Stupid question."

His eyes met mine. "Something happened the other day."

"With Iqbal?"

He frowned. "Yes. No. I'm not sure."

I sighed. "Tell me."

He tried on an ill-fitting smile. "I dunno. It's dumb. You'll think I'm crazy."

"'But you must be mad,'" I quoted. "'We're all mad here.'"

Unlike the Cheshire Cat's, his smile became a little more real as he quoted back: "'There's no use trying. One can't believe impossible things.'" His smiled cracked. "Maybe it was just the stress. Of everything. Of Iqbal. . . ."

My drink had arrived. I took a sip, let the bite and chill of it roll around on my tongue, swallowed. "Pete, I'm listening. You know I always will, no matter how crazy the thing you have to tell me." I said it, no matter how hurt I was that we weren't really friends any more.

His eyes were wet. "You remember Mrs. Richardson."

It wasn't a question. Pete and I had known each other since we were teenagers in high school. He was the first person I told outright that I wasn't a boy. He'd laughed it off, quite gently. But I'd never mentioned it to him again.

And of course I remembered that cunt. She shouldn't have been allowed near kids, much less allowed to foster young Pete. Meeting a foster kid had been quite the eye-opener for me. Meeting the spinning ball of hatred that was Mrs. Richardson made the skin on my arms crawl, made me almost grateful for my passive-aggressive mother and my transphobic dad.

I said, "One minute she'd be sweet as pie, the next she'd be raging."

"She wasn't always like that, though. At some point, she changed."

I hadn't known that. "Really? What turned her evil, then?"

"The other way round, Sal."

Good. I was back to being Sally, or as close as Pete would get to it. "Wait—you mean she used to be worse?"

He nodded. "When I was first placed with her, she'd come at me night and day. She said I was a lost cause, but she would whip me into shape. Once I laid the table with the knives and forks on the wrong side of the plates. She sent me to bed without dinner."

"Seriously?"

"She made me do all kinds of evening and weekend chores till I was so tired, I fell asleep on top of my homework. Then she punished me for getting bad grades. Took my socks away that fall and winter. Couple of my toes never recovered from the frostbite."

It felt like the bottom had dropped out of my belly. "We were friends! Why didn't you tell me?" The Mrs. Richardson I'd met mostly yelled a lot. Vile things, usually variants of "dumbass." And she'd refused to give permission for Pete to go on any school trips.

"I'd only just met you. It started happening in summer, when you were away at camp. And anyway, it didn't last long."

"Lasted long enough for you to get frostbite that winter."

He shrugged. "What good would telling you have done?"

"We could have told my folks, or the school! Someone would have gotten you out of there!" I was nearly shouting. People near us glanced at us, then looked away.

"You've never been a foster kid. More likely, no one would have believed us and the investigation would just have made her hate me even more."

All that time, he'd been suffering. And all this time, he'd kept his secret from me.

"She was careful to only hit me in places the bruises wouldn't be seen."

"Jesus." I sucked back more of my drink and waited for him

to continue. But he stayed silent. I prompted him: "What made her get nicer? Or at least, made her stop physically hurting you?"

"I've told you about my dad, right?"

Clearly he needed to change the subject. "Yeah, a bit." Pete's dad had raised him alone. Got hit by a car and killed when Pete was thirteen. That's how Pete had ended up in foster care.

"Dad used to let me read *Alice in Wonderland* to him. He took me fishing, worked on my science fair projects with me. He never raised a hand to me.

"I saw the accident, rode with Dad in the ambulance. He was bleeding, semi-conscious, but he held my hand till he couldn't any more. He kept saying, 'I'll come back to you, Petey. I have to look after you.' And then of course he didn't come back. He died. And I was sent to Mrs. Richardson." Pete clamped his hands around his drink. They were trembling a little. I wondered whether he'd even told Iqbal about Mrs. Richardson.

My drink had gone right through me, and I desperately needed to pee. I knew from past experience this place had segregated washrooms. That's why—or one of the reasons why—I'd stopped coming to this bar. I crossed my legs and leaned forward in my chair, as Pete clearly had more to say about that bloody bitch.

"One day, she was hitting me—on my legs—and I was trying to act like it wasn't hurting. She was pissed because of some damned thing she thought I'd done, I don't even re-member what. I do remember I was trying to tell her that I hadn't done it, and she was shouting, 'Children should be seen and not heard!'"

I stared at Pete, my mouth open in shock.

"Suddenly she stopped mid-swing, with her hand pulled up, like someone had grabbed her by the wrist. She opened her eyes wide and said, '*Petey*.' And . . . she stopped hitting me. She dropped to her knees to look at the bruises that were coming up on my thighs. And then she said the strangest thing."

"What?" I was trying hard to forget my twinging bladder. One of the two TERFy dykes had just gone to the washroom. The other was watching me, her lip curled in disgust.

"She said, 'What did she do to you?' You know, talking about herself in the third person? Then she went to hug me! That freaked me the fuck out. I pushed her away. She stood up, looked confused. She asked me where the kitchen was."

"In her own house? Was she having a stroke, or something?"

"Yeah, maybe. Iqbal was confused too, when he had his first stroke. . . ."

"Hey," I said, "Do you want to get out of here, just go home? Or come back to our place? We have a guest room, you could spend the night."

But Pete was looking off into the memory distance. He continued, "I pointed to where the kitchen was. She came back with cold water and paper towel. She dabbed my bruises and said she was sorry, that it was such a long way back and she'd brought the water as quickly as she could."

"Bitch was seriously crazy."

Pete had the waiter bring us refills. I hoped I could hold my water. In a pinch, I could dash back home, use the toilet there, be back in twenty, thirty minutes tops, and not risk being attacked for the unforgiveable crime of peeing in a public toilet.

"After that," said Pete, "I never knew whether I was going to get evil Mrs. Richardson or good Mrs. Richardson. It messed with my head. Sometimes she'd just sit in her armchair in front of the TV and mutter, like she was arguing with herself. And sometimes she'd just look scared out of her wits. I was so glad when I was legal to leave."

I smiled. "I was big-time envious of you, getting to be on your own when you were sixteen."

"You were an idiot, then."

"Yeah, probably."

"That was no picnic, either." He sipped his drink, then looked up. "I just remembered something. The day I left, I was just heading out the door when she put her hand on my shoulder. I nearly jumped out of my skin. She said, 'I'm sorry I couldn't look after you the whole time. It's such a long way round.' Then her hand fell away, and her face just changed. She stepped back. She watched me leave, and the look on her face was the most hatred I've ever had directed at me. And that's saying something. I scrambled down the driveway like the Devil was at my heels."

I shuddered. "Did you ever see her again?"

"Not her, no. Heard she'd jumped in front of a car, or something. Didn't care."

"Pete," I said gently, "you were telling me about Iqbal?"

He stared into his glass, spoke with his head still down. "We used to fight. Like, knockdown fistfights."

"Oh, no."

"'Fraid so. Blood was shed, there were trips to Emergency, the police were called."

"*Police?* To a fight between two brown men?"

"Yeah. It's a miracle we survived."

When one lives in a world in which large portions of it want one dead, every minute is a triumph, every breath a defiance, and, if one's jib is cut that way, every statement a manifesto.

The everyday vagaries of life and love are just writ that much larger, because they mean that much more. The game of "he said/he said" is raised to a level of artistry rivalled only by the sport of kings. Every breakup is forever, because love may never find one ever again. Every new lover becomes one's whole life, because one is stealing love from the jaws of hatred. What T-shirt to wear with the perfect jeans to go clubbing is almost as brutally important as what words to write on one's placard to attend that demonstration against legalizing faith-based homophobia. "I'm so sorry."

"Don't be sorry. It stopped, all the violence between us. One day, Iqbal took his hands from around my throat—"

"Pete!"

"—and he looked at his hands as though he'd never seen them before. He said, 'No more. I'm not going to fight you anymore.' I mean, it didn't end right away. For one thing, I wasn't ready to stop. Didn't know how, really. But Iqbal really meant it. He'd changed. Eventually he got me to go to counselling with him. And bit by bit, we figured shit out. Figured out how to be good to each other." Pete sobbed, once, so loudly that people three tables over stopped to look our way. "God, Sally, I miss him so much."

"I know, honey." I took his hand in mine. He jumped at my touch. I tried not to feel hurt.

"You know the last thing he said to me?"

I shook my head.

"He said, 'I found my way home to you, Petey. I looked after you. I got better at it, so that I could be with you all the time.' He went unconscious after that, and was gone by the next morning."

"He loved you very much. That wasn't strange at all."

He nodded absently, then pulled his hand away to pick his glass up. He had a sip. "Okay," he said. "I suppose. But here's the thing; only my dad ever called me Petey."

I tried to concentrate through the yammering of my bladder. "No, that's not right. Didn't you say that Mrs. Richardson did?"

"Once. The day she stopped hitting me."

"And Iqbal?"

"Once. The last time he was conscious." Pete's hands started shaking so badly that he had to set the glass down. He put his hands in his lap. "So what I'm really asking myself is: who was I married to all those years?"

Something squirmed in the pit of my belly. How could he even think—? "Pete. . . ," I whispered.

He jumped to his feet. "I'm sorry, Sal. It's just been so hard the last couple of days. Losing Iqbal, the funeral, all those people to be polite to while . . ." He stopped, his face pulled into the lineaments of grief. "My head's just been full of all these weird thoughts."

"I understand," I murmured. But I didn't. "You need to be gentle with yourself this next little while."

"Let me get the check." He put some bills on the table.

"Okay, thanks, but first I just need to . . ." I stood, clamping down hard on my aching bladder. Another reason to be thankful I'd diligently done all those post-surgery kegels.

Pete sighed, as one does when one is about to say something difficult for others to hear. "It's just that . . . well, Mrs. Richardson, Iqbal; people around me keep turning into someone else. You used to be Jack; now you're Sally."

The cold burn of betrayal and erasure was just about to tsunami over me, scouring me from skin to bone, when he got a strange look in his eye. In a clear voice, he said, "But Jack is just what people called you. I finally figured it out. You were always Sally. You have always been exactly who you are right now."

I can be an emo bitch sometimes. When I started weeping, he pulled me into his arms. "Sally, I'm sorry I've been such a dick." For the first time in years, my friend and I held each other like the close companions we used to be.

And then I really, really had to go. I waited, hot-footing, till I was as sure as I could be that there was no one in the Women's. Pete stood outside the door painted with the stick figure lady in a triangle skirt until I exited safely. He walked me home, hugged me again on the street outside my apartment building. I told him I'd check in on him tomorrow, waved goodbye as he headed off in the direction of the subway station.

Age and a track record of survival can bring poise to a life lived cheek by jowl with the possibility of danger. Nevertheless, one is always watchful for that slight shift, the moment when a situation turns.

That new look in Pete's eye, the complete change of demeanour. And wasn't that the first time, he'd called me Sally? Not Jack-er-Sal. Not Sal. Sally.

Broad Dutty Water: A Sunken Story

De river ben come down
And how you cross over
De broad dutty water?

These are some of the lyrics from a Jamaican folk song
I remember from my girlhood. It's a call-and-response
song in which the main singer is telling the story of
making a dangerous crossing on foot through a rushing
river swollen by flooding. I cannot find an author for
it. When I was young, the singer's feat sounded like no
big deal to me; wow, they walked across the shallows of
a river made brown by churned-up silt. Didn't sound
very dangerous. Now, though, some decades later, I've
seen the devastation that flooding can do, the deaths it
can cause. And like the rest of the world, I'm watching
global warming make it so much worse. I moved back
to Canada in 2021 and settled in Vancouver, British
Columbia. That year, a minor tornado touched down
on the University of British Columbia campus (unheard
of). The rains brought such bad flooding that highways

*were turned into canyons, livestock drowned, and salm-
on fisheries were contaminated. For awhile, Vancouver
was cut off from the rest of the country for overland
travel. The only road route was a small one that led
through the U.S. and back into Canada. Vancouver
used to have a temperate climate. Now, subzero winter
temperatures have become commonplace, as have summer heat waves, life-threatening in a city where homes
were not built for cooling.*

*A little while ago, I was talking to Barbados author
Karen Lord. We discovered that as Caribbean authors
who set stories in the future, we've both found ourselves
preoccupied with ocean-level rise. We're already seeing
the effects of larger storm surges and bigger hurricanes.
What will the low-lying areas of our birth region be
like five, ten, twenty years in the future? Clearly, that
was on my mind when I wrote "Broad Dutty Water."
Caribbean people are ingenious, as people everywhere
are. I tapped into some of that to imagine a method of
survival. Also on my mind were the swimming oceanside
wild pigs of Bermuda, because cool.*

*Some people have criticized the story for skipping
past the potential resolution to the story problem in a
quick half sentence. That's fair. It would also have been
the beginning of a whole new story, wrenching the current story arc out of true and shifting the focus from a
story of one character's personal journey to the beginning
of a global shift in attitude and government policy. Science fiction is very fond of imagining grand gestures to
fix the world at a swoop. It's a favourite narrative from
a position of relative entitlement, but it's also one of the*

things I love about this genre. Yet it's also possible to write stories in this mode that aren't about the conquering hero saving the world, but about the person living in a besieged community who's beginning to contemplate that along with the real and necessary daily survival, they and their community might find a way to make change on a larger scale.

Don't worry, though. I wasn't blind to the possibilities of the world I created in "Broad Dutty Water." Fellow artist David Findlay and I have written a treatment for some kind of extended media piece that's set in that world. No idea what will happen with it yet. But it exists.

"GET IN, LICKCHOP." Jacquee lifted her pig into the main cabin of Uncle Silvis's ultralight she'd borrowed from home.

Lickchop merely grunted, *Chow* via the vocoder illegally implanted in his scalp. Jacquee didn't know who'd done that to him; is so she'd found him last year, a half-dead lump of throw-weh, unconscious and sinking fast in the centre of a medical waste trash vortex about seventy nmi offshore of the Grande Soufrière false atoll that loomed over sunken Guadeloupe. No one back home could figure out why the vocoder had a ring of tiny rods, each a couple millimetres long, sticking out the top of Lickchop's skull. Jacquee called it his tiara. Lickchop didn't much use the vocoder, except to demand chow. At the moment, he was eagerly paddling his stubby legs in the air.

"I know, sweetness," Jacquee said to him. "I'm impatient,

too." She was mad to try out her brand new wetware. Dr. Lin had said she should wait a week, but he always exaggerated that bullshit. He was an old boyfriend of Uncle Silvis's. As hospitals became too overwhelmed with flood, plague, and starvation victims to function adequately, he'd moved his surgery practice to his home. Five years now Jacquee had been going to him. He'd replaced her left elbow after she splintered it on a dive in a dead coral reef. He kept her taz supplied with antibiotics he mixed up in his kitchen. She regularly brought him gifts of food her taz bred. Some of those were illegal to have, but he'd never turned her in to the World Bioheritage enforcers.

As soon as Jacquee put Lickchop down on the floor of the ultralight's tiny cabin, he trotted click-click over to the spongiform food puzzle she'd bolted to the floor in one corner. He stuck his snout into it and began happily rooting for the algae pellets she'd made and tucked inside.

Activity on the makeshift post-Inundation dock bustled all around them: people with their belongings on their backs hustling from the mainland to the water along the rocky wooden boards of the makeshift bridge over the new wetlands; boats and catamarans docking and getting underway; people shouting orders; the air-filling duppy moans of ships' horns; the oily fish-swamp stink of water polluted by gas engines. The original land was somewhere below them, swallowed by the polluted black waters of the risen ocean. Nobody was really sure what Florida town or city they were floating above; catastrophic flooding and the resulting seismic activity had changed shorelines too much, and were still doing so.

Jacquee clambered behind Lickchop into the small cabin of her ultralight. Her knapsack dragged at her shoulders, though it really wasn't plenty heavy. She was just a little tired from the surgery. She straightened up, and her world spun backward. Vertigo. She clutched for one of the handstraps in the ceiling. She was a bit unsteady on her pins after the slicendice Dr. Lin had performed on her the day before. She should have stayed in his spare bedroom one more day, to recover from the laparoscopic surgery and get a bit more training in how to use the wetware he'd just implanted in her brain. But two days a-landlock was enough. She and Lickchop needed to get home, back to the sea and their taz massive-them in the Jamdown Ark. The floating platform on which her community lived had been travelling for weeks to get to the next berth on its annual route, the one east of the Caribbean crescent. Now it was time to reestablish their vertical farm. This week, Jacquee would be helping to lay out the floating grid of plastic pipes with the newest kelp seedlings sprouted along their lengths. Then there'd be mussel socks to attach to the grid and lower into the water, plus the cages stocked with clam and oyster seeds. She liked this part of the endless round of tasks it took to keep the taz functioning. She got to freedive amongst the hanging fronds of kelp, swerving around the vertical cooling rods that chilled the ocean water passing through them to keep the kelp at optimum temperature. She was up to five minutes of being able to hold her breath. Uncle Silvis could do seven; Plaidy who lived with her children and her man five habitats over on the taz was the current record-holder; almost nine minutes under the water before she would faint and have to be pulled out.

Jacquee pulled the ultralight's cabin door shut and looked through the porthole. So much waste being spat out all around her; a treasure trove. "Lickchop," she said as she went to top up the pig's water dispenser, "Give our taz two days here, and yuh would see how much we could salvage!"

The pig, busy filling his belly, ignored her. She got to work locking the lid on his stale litter box, opening a fresh one and dampening the peristaltic pad. A-pure truth she was talking. It would be easy for them to strain oil and microplastics out of the sludgy dockside water. Scoop up the dead birds and fish floating stink on the surface, render them into fat and ash. Sell all of that back to the factory suppliers, fund ongoing taz maintenance for weeks.

She secured the door open to Lickchop's well-padded crate, made from a large grocery shopping cart she'd traded for a few months ago with one youth in a passing taz called Travellers' Green. She'd given him an empty lard tub of dried coconut meal and a handful of freeze-dried chiton meat for it. And though the youth had kept asking her, she hadn't told him where she'd found the forlorn piece of rock sticking up out of the sea that still had chitons living on it. Not that it mattered; next time she went back, there weren't any, just scum floating around the base of the rock. Salt water was so acid these days that it was removing the calcium carbonate so many now near-extinct sea creatures relied on to build their shells. How long since she'd tasted lobster or crab?

She did a quick check of the repair patches bolted onto the ultralight. Uncle Silvis had printed the body of the aircraft in pieces from bio-polymers her taz cultured from marine algae. The assembled ultralight had held up well for the past few years, but it was soon going to be time to feed it back to the algae. Uncle Silvis kept joking that it was now more patch than plane. By now, Uncle Silvis had probably realized that she'd taken it for a ride. There was going to be some music to face when she got back home.

She was little bit lightheaded after her flight prep, but never mind; time to go. She patted Lickchop, went forward to the flight deck, and closed the cabin door behind her. No control tower to radio to, nowhere to register a flight path or wait for an all-clear to take-off. Everyone used visual flight rules this near to a port; keep your eyes peeled like johncrow head and don't get too close to any other craft.

Pretty soon, she was kiting near soundlessly twelve hundred feet above sea level. World Bioheritage couldn't come after her once she reached her taz. Not legally, anyway. Land-liberated micronations were a protected category. Though now that the open oceans had been declared a protected heritage site, World-bio porkpies sometimes got overeager and took the chance of invading tazes, hoping they could make an arrest under claim of defacing an international heritage.

The ultralight console began an insistent beeping. Jacquee opened her eyes, checked the readout, corrected the ultralight's flight so that its right wing was no longer dipping downward.

The intercom clicked on. "Yes, Lickchop?" Jacquee responded.

She should never have taught the pig how to use the inter-com, much less have rewired the controls to low enough on the wall for him to reach. But he got lonely back there in the cabin on long trips. She couldn't have him in the cockpit. He'd be a menace.

Columbus considered it to be the fairest isle that eyes have beheld, said Lickchop.

The skin on Jacquee's arms sprang out in goosebumps. She stared at the receiver in her hand. That hadn't come from Lickchop's limited vocabulary range. "Is who back there?" she barked into the receiver.

No answer.

"Assata," she said, "automatic pilot, current course heading."

Yes, pilot, replied the ultralight's A.I. Jacquee leapt out of her seat and snatched up the cricket bat she kept behind the door. She threw the door open and stepped into the cabin. Lickchop was dozing in his crate. He didn't even have the TV on. And the intercom hadn't been activated. "Wah gwan?" Jacquee muttered to herself. Frowning, she returned to the cockpit. True, she was feeling not quite herself. Dr. Lin had said a few people developed mild sensory hallucinations as this kind of wetware established its pathways in the brain. Looked like she was one of them. Cho.

But Dr. Lin had said they were temporary. Push come to shove, she could have Assata fly them home. Uncle Silvis had grumbled when she'd installed it—he thought Jacquee's love of bootleg tech was an addiction—but now he used Assata, too. He kept threatening to change its name, 'ascording to how the real Assata never took a rassclaat order from nobody.' But he hadn't done so yet. The list of things Uncle Silvis planned to get to someday was ever-changing and never-ending.

Her headphones crackled to life, causing a pain-pulse to start throbbing along the top of her skull. "Jaks! A-you that?"

Oi. Time to face the music with Uncle Silvis. "Come in, Tay-zone 67," she replied. "A-who this?"

"Is Kobe." It usually was, if it was a matter of telecommunications. "Yuh business conclude?" he asked.

"Ee-hee." No need to tell him about her worrisome symptoms. She'd be all right. She basked in the familiar sound leaking from Kobe's side; children yelling as they played all through the complex.

Kobe said, "You enjoyed your visit to landlock?"

"So you know is there I went?"

"Cho. Is who you think you talking to? Of course I know!"

"The whole rahtid place don't move!" This she knew how to do; to cover over her doubts with humour. "They pretend they do; everything rushing all around you; cars and trains and people. Everybody trying to keep things going fast just so them don't haffe realize that them NAH GO NOWHERE!"

Kobe laughed. "Well, yuh know what dem seh: if yuh worl' nah rock, it a-'tan 'till."

"My legs couldn't adjust, even after three days. With no water jostling beneath my feet, I was walking like I was drunk. How people live like that, Kobe?"

"After you barely been living ten years at sea," he teased. "I know you didn't forget so soon. Listen, we picking up a light breeze. We gwine ride it; gie de sea under we some time to freshen herself up. Change your course heading minus 20 degrees, so you could catch up."

"Seen. And I coming home with a new toy in my head." She glanced at her console. "Twenty minutes."

From her headphones came the sound of a familiar voice: "Kobe, hand me that blasted microphone. Jacquee? A-you that?"

Jacquee sighed. "Yes, Uncle Silvis."

"Jimmy text me to say you leave his surgery too soon. You all right, Jacquee? Why you went to Dr. Lin? Something happen to you?"

So worried the old man sounded. He wasn't even her real uncle. That's just what everyone called him. And didn't he know by now she could look after herself? She replied, "Yeah, man. Just a little mod. Help me see better in muh—murky water." Even just saying the phrase made her belly twist, every time.

"More bootleg tech?" said Uncle Silvis. "And in your head this time? What the rass Jimmy was thinking, letting you talk him into doing something like that?"

Jacquee tried for a light tone. "Better him than some back-awall operator with no training, nah true?"

"Jacquee, this is foolishness! When you going to start acting like you have a brain in your head?"

The pounding in her head increased. "Jesus Christ," she barked, "if you going to carry on like that, maybe I won't come home at all! Maybe I gwine right back to landlock, where I belong!" She cut off the connection before he could reply, and sat stewing—kissing her teeth and muttering under her breath about interfering, over-protective . . .

There was the thunderhead Kobe had talked about, looming up ahead. It would bring a storm surge. No problem for Jamdown Ark. Its large, flexible base—a neural matrix of algal polymers extruded in a ring shape—would just rise and fall with the swells. The sway would make it a bit wobbly underfoot for a few hours, is all.

A decade ago when Jacquee was still living a-landlock, rainy season might mean some flooding. Nowadays, every downpour was a tropical storm, and every storm saw the waters rise more and destroy more land. At least there were no hurricanes due for another few months. The old-time stories talked about the devastation of Category 5s. But the classifications had had to be revised. In these days Category 5 was common, and the new Category 6 was a banshee-shrieking horror that could tear away coastlines permanently, eat small countries whole.

Uncle Silvis insisted that the aftermath of storm surges was the best time to go collecting. Worldbio porkpies didn't patrol during storms, and the storm waters churned interesting stuff up from the depths. That's how Jacquee had stumbled upon the chitons; clambering on a slippery thumb of rock jutting out of the ocean. The storm that had just washed over it had deposited caches of glass jetsam, weathered and rounded over decades into gleaming lumps by being tumbled along the ocean floor. She would keep the prettiest, most beadlike pieces to make jewellery with for market. The rest could be sold to recyclers. Prying the barnacles out of the rock had broken a good hunting knife, but Uncle Silvis had been delighted to find that Jacquee's haul included twenty-three of them she'd kept alive in a little tub of sea water. "Viable gametes probably still dey inside," he'd said. "Good for you." He'd extracted some sperm and ova from a few of the chitons and cryopreserved the gametes in DMSO, cooled then stored in a liquid nitrogen flask.

Maybe they could find a way to add chitons to the vertical marine farm suspended underwater in the doughnut-hole centre of Jamdown Ark. They might be good for chowder.

Blasted man. She wasn't going to let him spoil her fun with her new mod. "Assata," she said, "take the helm. Maintain course."

Yes, pilot, said Assata.

Jacquee flicked on the intercom. She needed some company. Lickchop was singing along with some TV show contestant. Jacquee could hear the show in the background, but the loudest sound was Lickchop. He was making excited squeal/grunts that his vocoder was struggling to render into some approximation of human speech; Jacquee's best guess was *Shake that t'ing, Miss / Oonuh betta shake. . . .* An oldie but a goodie. Wasn't helping her aching head, though. "Lickchop!" she barked.

The "singing" stopped. *What Jah-kay want?* he responded. "Turn down the TV for a second, nuh man?"

He did. Then he was silent, waiting for her to answer his question. She didn't even self know what she wanted from the pig.

Just his attention. Ongle that. Lickchop didn't pass judgement. She rummaged in her knapsack for the bootleg addy she'd been carrying around for months. "He think I so foolish," she muttered to Lickchop. "Like I can't think for myself. Gwine show him."

Don't think you foolish.

"Not you, Lickchop; Uncle Silvis." She hadn't been sure she was going to try it. But she was a hard-back woman who would make her own decisions. So now she was going to see if the bootleg addy would pair with her new mod.

The woman she'd bought the addy from in the mainland market had said, "Medically non-intrusive for sure, darling." Then she'd tapped the side of her head. "You already have wetware installed, right? Maybe to correct myopia? Just piggyback it onto that. So easy, it's sleazy."

Well, she hadn't had any wetware. Not then, anyway. But she'd been thinking to get some anyway, and now she had. The mod was well natty on its own; enhanced vision would help direct her through murky, particulate-heavy water and sharpen her proprioception. Accomplished via some process she didn't really understand. Something about ninety percent modifications to her DNA and ten percent implanted hardware. Didn't matter.

A pop song cover came pouring out through Jacquee's headphones. Lickchop had clearly decided the conversation was over. She grimaced and turned the sound off.

She got the addy out of her knapsack. A matchbox-sized plastic box, standard 3-D print white and near featureless, but for a readout window and a couple of buttons. She unfolded the piece of paper with the instructions written on it in fading umpteenth-generation print. They were easy enough to follow.

In a few seconds, the readout was flashing "ready" in squared-off green letters. Addy successfully onboarded! Her brain felt a little . . . itchy. That was the only way to describe it.

The headache scoured the inside of her skull, making her wince. She should be lying in Dr. Lin's lavender-scented guest bedroom with a soft mask over her eyes, wearing a cooled gel skullcap and gently putting her aching brain through the exercises that would, in about a week, fine-tune her skill with the mod. She closed her eyes for some relief.

The discomfort receded. She took a breath. Focused her mind the way Dr. Lin had shown her. She was supposed to wait a couple more days before trying out the commands, but she summoned the wetware anyway. Gave it the "standby" command, then squinched her lower left eyelid. That was the action she'd chosen to activate the addy. The headache became a shout of pain. She did her best to ignore it. She felt/heard the internal click as the addy connected with the ultralight's controls. Success! Now she could pilot the ultralight hands-free. Assata was great for uneventful flight paths, but not for the myriad split-second decisions of flying manually. So often Jacquee had wished she could do that without having to lay her hands on the controls all the time. "Assata, switch to manual control."

Yes, pilot.

Jacquee called up the addy's display. Telemetry danced across the upper left-hand corner of her mind's eye. Red, yellow, and green images on a black background. She felt/saw the ultralight's controls. Tasted them, too. Like goat-head soup mixed with pineapple and toothpaste. She gagged as she fought to do the mental twitch that turned the gain down. The ultralight swung dizzyingly to the left. Carefully, Jacquee got it back on track. She experimented for a while with pitch, yaw, speed. Pretty soon, she felt comfortable enough to climb to two thousand feet to get above the storm. Grinning, she frolicked the aircraft among the clouds.

Oh, shit. The telemetry was signalling that she'd dipped too low. She was tipping them into the thunderhead. With the sickly swanning motion of a piece of paper drifting down from a height, they sank into the storm cloud. Like a truck on a quarry road, they dugga-duggaed through turbulence. A buffet of wind jerked the ultralight sideways. Rain beat fists against the window screen, hammered the ultralight with a roar that made bile rise in her throat. She spat it down the front of her sweatshirt, kept trying for the right combo of commands to de-couple the addy from the ultralight's controls. A storm like this could literally tear the ultralight in two.

Automatically, she reached for the controls, just as the craft hit an air pocket and dropped so fast that Jacquee's butt lifted out of the chair. The heel of her hand hit multiple buttons and levers.

She didn't know which ones. Panicked, she tried to use the mental commands instead, succeeded only in jamming the whole system up. "Assata!" she yelled, "Take the con!"

Not possible, pilot, the plane replied calmly. *Please disengage override.*

"I can't!"

The rain had become hail, slamming like fast balls against the hull.

The ultralight's nose dipped at a vomitous pitch and exited the cloud layer. There was a mountain top floating in the dark swells of the ocean below her, like a meringue in wine. For a brief second she thought she'd pulled the ultralight out of its dive, but it just. kept. falling. She fought to stay conscious during the plummet, tried pushing one combo after another of buttons that now made no sense to her confused brain. She could hear Lickchop's fear squeal from the cabin behind her. G-forces pressed her into her chair like a ripe mango beneath a boot. Dirty-blue water getting closer and closer. "Assata," Jacquee yelled, "Controlled descent! Parallel to the shoreline ahead!"

Please disengage override.

"I still fucking can't figure it out!" yelled Jacquee.

Then I suggest you deploy your parachute. Ditch at one thousand feet.

The ultralight continued its dizzying descent. The silence was eerie, except for the tinny music of Lickchop's TV show coming from her discarded headphones. *Shake that thing, Miss . . .*

Jacquee scrabbled for the life jacket with its attached chute. She pulled the package out from beneath the seat, mentally rehearsing how to put it on.

She only had one on board. And the ultralight had two passengers. "Pussyclaat, batty-hole. . . ," she swore.

She undid her seatbelt, stood against the steep downward angle of the ultralight, and clawed her way through the door, into the main cabin. She rushed to Lickchop's crate, yanked its door open. He was crouched inside, his eyes rolling in terror. *Fallingfalling,* said his vocoder. He tunneled his way into her arms. He was shivering. He had shit inside his crate; she could smell it. And sympathize.

"You gonna be okay," she lied. She had no way of knowing that. She clutched Lickchop against her chest and struggled into the life vest, wrapping it round both of them.

Nonono, said Lickchop. He fought and kicked. *No leash.*

"Is not a leash. Shut up."

In his struggling, Lickchop slashed her forearm open with a back trotter.

"Ow! Fuck!" Blood was seeping through the sleeve of her jacket. But still she held Lickchop tightly.

Twelve hundred feet, said Assata. *The aircraft is losing altitude too quickly. It will break up on the coral formation at crash site. On my mark, release the hatch, open the door, and jump.*

Jacquee stood near the hatch, her hand on the handle. She knew what she had to do. Open the hatch outward. Leap out of the plane. Open the first 'chute once she was clear of it. Steer herself and Lickchop down, hopefully onto the dry land of the little island below them. She didn't even know what country it used to be.

Eleven hundred feet, said Assata. *Mark. Exit the aircraft now. Exit the aircraft now. Exit the aircraft now.*

Jacquee felt her kidneys clench, her gut knot. Everything about her body was telling her this was a bad idea. But she pushed down on the handle, leaned against the door to push it open.

Mistake. A buffeting wind slammed the door outward on its hinge to bang against the ultralight's carriage. She didn't have to jump; the force of the wind yanked her out of the ultralight, into a heels-over-head somersault. She saw the bottom edge of the open hatch, but couldn't avoid it. Her head crashed against it, then she was out.

The day the waters had swept over the house in the valley where teenaged Jacquee lived with her parents, she'd been in the living room, dozing over her history homework in the big Berbice lounge chair. She woke when water poured over shoulders, carrying the chair along in the surge. Coughing, she struggled to her knees in the chair. The back half of the house was gone, open to an iron-coloured sky and an avalanche of angry brown water where neighbours' houses had been. The roar of wind and water had been like a train coming through. She'd yelled for her Mummy and Daddy. They had been in the back yard, bringing in the lawn chairs and picnic umbrella so they wouldn't blow away in the storm. There was no sign of them. The river maelstrom had claimed the yard, and the rest of the house was crumbling into it, fast. Her mind couldn't take it in. She waded from room to room, splashing and coughing in the gritty, bitter water, calling and calling for her parents. No answer. Something long and snaky, concealed in the torrent, went whipping along the front of her, wrapped itself around her ankle, and held her fast. Then the water had fountained over her, filling her mouth. It had felt like a long, pounding forever of terror before she'd been able to bend and unsnarl the thing from her ankle. Its hard metal nose told her that it was their garden hose. Her parents had probably brought it indoors.

With a nail-bending screech, the roof of the house tore away. The house was disintegrating. She had to go. The garage was above the house, a bit farther along the uphill grade. The structure itself was gone, but the waters hadn't reached the car yet. She gave thanks her parents had recently keyed the car lock to her finger-prints. By the time she'd fought her way snotting and sobbing to the car, the sewage-tainted water was up to its tyre tops and she had lost her sweatpants and one shoe. Crouched on the car's bonnet was their cat Smarty Pants. She was bone-dry as God's sense of humour, her lemon eyes wide in terror. By some miracle, the car started. Jacquee headed for even higher ground. She picked up six more shellshocked survivors on the way. They made it to the stadium, which had been converted into an emergency centre. She spent two weeks there, being drip-fed antibiotics and shitting bloody e. Coli flux. That's where the man she would come to know as Uncle Silvis found her and a handful of other people willing to form a taz and take to sea with him. Yes, he'd already ordered a taz platform. It would be grown and ready in a couple of weeks. Yes, he knew how to manage himself on the water and could teach them. Yes, she could bring Smarty Pants.

The first month at sea she huddled in her bunk while others were busy setting up the habitats of the newly grown taz. She fought seasickness while grief raged through her. Wha' mek Mummy and Daddy dead, but she still alive? And every night of the decade since, she would dream of struggling in rushing, murky water as snakes wrapped around her ankles and pulled her down to drown.

She was . . . dizzy. Spinning along every axis possible. A keening shriek filled her thoughts. She told herself she had to open her eyes. Herself disagreed.

The keening was her. She was screaming. She closed her mouth. The screaming stopped. That slight bit of control made room for her to take more. She opened her eyes, and nearly began screaming again. The world was whipping around edge over edge, twisting; sky to sea to mountains, whup whup whip. She craned her neck upward, looking for the parachute. It hadn't inflated. It was flapping in circles above her, flaccid as a used rubber, dragging behind her and Lickchop as they plummeted.

She was still holding Lickchop. Her thoughts were going so slow!

What had Kobe said in his flight training? "If you can't pilot it, ditch it to rass."

Ditch . . . how? Yes. There should be a lever at the front of the jacket. She had to squeeze Lickchop even tighter to reach it. If the pig protested, she couldn't hear it above the wind whooshing in her ears. She found the lever. Grasped it. Pulled downward. She felt the tug of the first parachute releasing her, then the sharp yank upward as the second chute deployed. It was smaller, round rather than the rectangle shape of the first one. It began rapidly filling with air. But would it be enough? She was coming in hot. The parachute was only half full, and couldn't be steered like the first one could. The vista surrounding her had rapidly gone from a wide glimpse of Earth's curvature, sky above and sea below with patches of brown earth barely poking like noses above the water, to sea with a scrim of land too far out of reach in front of her, to just sea, then waves became apparent, and then she hit the surface of the water, feet first. But she hadn't kept her feet properly together. She felt her right ankle as wrench she plunged into the drink.

Lickchop couldn't hold his breath!

He could swim, though. Loved it, in fact. She pulled him out of the life jacket and let him go, knowing his rotund, potbellied self would pop up to the surface.

And still she cannonballed downward, despite the life vest. She could do this. She had practiced holding her breath. Her vision tunneled and her head felt light and airless as the space between stars. She could barely restrain the instinct to take a big gasp. The second she slowed enough to make it possible, she began frantically frog-swimming back up to the life-giving air. Adrenaline rush kept the pain of her ankle at bay.

Her head broke the surface. She sucked in air. She was alive. "Lickchop!" she yelled, spinning in a circle. No pig. The rope-tentacled mass of the second parachute was floating nearby, dragging her along. Lickchop didn't appear to be on it. She pressed the button on her vest that disengaged the parachute from her. It obediently began shrinking and rolling itself up for transport. Jacquee swam around a few strokes, calling Lick-chop's name. She dove briefly, but couldn't see him beneath the surface, either. He was gone.

Reaction to her close call was setting in, and she wasn't safe yet. She could drown or be attacked by sharks or stung by some of the nastier jellyfish before getting to safety. Was that going to happen to Lickchop? Had it already? Sobbing, exhausted, she turned and began swimming for the beach, towing the parachute roll awkwardly. About a half mile farther along the shore were the smoking pieces of the wreckage of her ultralight. She couldn't business with that now. Out of the water first. See to that ankle. Maybe rig up a canoe and go looking for Lickchop.

She had reached the breakers. They were big today, in the wake of the passing storm. A good ten, twelve feet. She swam and body-surfed her way through them, diving beneath them when necessary. It was a mercy the water was cool enough to numb her ankle little bit.

She didn't deserve mercy.

One more crashing wave shoved her closer to the shore. Jacquee's feet hit the bottom with a thud. She shouted at the jarring of her injured ankle. She staggered the rest of the way through a porridge of roiled-up, mealy sand and suspicious solids that banged against her legs and twice knocked her off her feet to splash into the nasty water. She hated being in water she couldn't see through. The second time, a big branch scraped painfully across her body. It snagged in her vest. She had to yank frantically at the branch. It tore free, dragging her life vest off with it, and sped into the undertow, heading out to sea. Great. The survival kit and tracking device had been packed into that vest. Home didn't even know she was down. Would the tracker even still be broadcasting by the time they figured it out?

Once she was out of the surf, Jacquee half-hopped onto shore, groaning. When she could no longer hop, she got down on hands and knees and crawled like any baby, dragging the wadded-up parachute behind her. Salt water stung inside her nose, driven into her sinuses by the speed with which she'd plunged into the water. Never mind. Her own snot would flush them soon enough. She was bawling and coughing at the same time. Lickchop had been in her care. How she could go and do him so? Uncle Silvis was forever telling her not to take him on her trips. But she hadn't listened. Losing beings she loved to the water; that was what she did best.

Tainted sand and pieces of sodden, rotted branches gave way to rockstones and tangles of stinking seaweed harried by sandflies. The beach was lined by what was probably seagrape bushes. Frayed and bent, their slimy stems dragged on the sand. Their broad, heart-shaped leaves were yellowed. There was a handful of the usual coconut trees arched over the beach, but their fronds drooped wetly. That meant that now that Earth's waters were rising higher than most had predicted, this beach was regularly completely covered by the sea. Jacquee had to get to higher ground. And she couldn't crawl the whole way.

She rolled to a sitting position and inspected her ankle. It was already puffy, but didn't seem broken.

A patch of sand in her peripheral vision writhed. But when she looked good at it, it wasn't moving. Jacquee scooted backward away from it. Since that day with the garden hose, she couldn't abide anything snakelike.

Out of her eye-corner another patch of sand squirmed. Again it was still when she looked at it. She thought she heard someone say, *It's all good. Just turn.* . . . She snapped her head round in the direction of the voice. No one.

Although she was dripping wet, heat flushed over her, like being splashed with warm water. The world started to wobble on its axis. Her ears were suddenly ringing, the tinny sound occasionally resolving into a whisper of not-words as her brain tried to make sense of the racket. And she was shivering. Bloody hell. There were no snakes in the sand. Leaving Dr. Lin's before she had healed, landing-up in unsterile water . . . she'd picked up some kind of bug, and now she was delirious. And her mouth was dry. All that salt water had her dehydrated.

She took stock as best she could, while her head rang like Sunday-go-to-meeting and the world got farther and farther away. . . . Penknife still in her front jeans pocket. Cut a piece from her parachute to make a solar still, throw the rest of the parachute over a branch to make a tent. She was a thikk gyal, wouldn't need food for weeks. Felt like her fever was rising, though. She needed clean water now, but the still would take hours to generate it. And what about predatory animals on this island?

Sea water splashed her feet. The tide was rising. She had to get above the shoreline, quick.

Give it up to me. . . .

She found a seagrape bush that had a branch long and thick enough. She tore the branch off to use as a crutch. Last minute, she thought to grab up a discarded PET bottle from the jetsam tumbling in the incoming water. She began the trek to drier ground.

Hot day. Jacquee was used to sea breezes playing over and through Jamdown Ark. Landlock felt stifling to her nowadays. Especially today. Is fever that? She didn't know. Her jeans and sweatshirt were mostly dry. Scratchy sea salt powdered her face and hands. Her clothes were stiff with it. It weighed down the parachute roll. She limped along, leaning on the stick. The pain in her ankle first went numb, then came back shrieking with each step. Flashes of light at her eye corners. Smarty Pants on the deck of the taz outside the habitat they shared with Uncle Silvis, purring and chowing down on algae protein pellets. But her cat was long gone, dead peacefully in her sleep at a ripe old age.

Voiceless voices. A ghost of Lickchop's de-modulated vocoder demanding, *Chow, Jacquee. Chow.* Jacquee kissed her teeth. Lickchop couldn't say her name smooth so. Always hesitated between one syllable and the next.

So of course the next thing was that she felt he was trotting beside her in the screaming hot sun, berating her for letting him die. She started arguing with him. *The calculus of dampness*, she said, *eating along the rimrock*. She briefly came back to herself, half-remembering the words she'd just muttered, vaguely aware they were nonsense. Then she was back in the fever dream.

Lickchop floated in the air, on his back, gnawing at a snake with brass fangs. It hissed and spit and tried to wrap itself around Lickchop, who calmly sucked it up like a strand of sea grass.

She caromed off a knee-height rock, hissed as she jammed her injured foot into the sand to prevent a fall. Two-handed,

tilted forward from the waist, she hung onto the branch she
was using to help herself walk. Bone-tired. She straightened up.
One foot forward, then the next one. Repeat.

There was a water-trickle sound, different than the rhythmic
roar of the seashore. She tried to focus, to see ahead of her, but
it was all delusion, her afflicted brain telling itself gigo stories.
Through it all, the one constant was the tuneless piano-plink
of water. She stumbled in the direction of the sound. Throat
parched. Fever rising. Even as she swam through imaginary
kelp fronds, ate a bat sandwich, won a not-game of dominoes
with a not-Silvis who was chanting the wrong words from the
book of Revelations while he silently slapped the tiles down
onto the rickety wooden table between them, she knew she had
to hydrate, soon.

Jacquee's eyes opened briefly on . . . a river? Weeds around
its edges
Lilies at the brink
Even some seagulls wheel-and-turning above it
Odourous indeed must be the mead
Some struggling but living sea-grape bushes
And sugar-sweet their sap
Hush, she told her dreaming brain. You can't drink that.
You don't know what kinda parasites inna it. You should dig a
solar still. Wait till some clean water condenses into it.

Her gritty, obstinate throat impelled her forward. She dimly
knew she was on her belly, face nearly in the water. Then she
was scooping brackish water up with the PET bottle, bringing
it to her mouth and drinking deep.

———————

Uncle Silvis had told her his dream often enough. Of the smog levels gradually falling. Of Earth's climates returning to cooler levels. Of the land reappearing.

But the world had lost so much. The Gulf Coast. The eastern seaboard. The Amazon River basin. Most of southeast Asia had dived beneath the waves. And the Pacific Island nations. Refugees, misery, sickness everywhere. And the grief. A whole planet keening, mourning.

Jacquee slapped the side of her neck, hard. She woke to find it was pitch-night. She was scraping away the mosquito she'd squashed against her neck in her sleep. She was sprawled by the waterside, curled around the plastic bottle. Her head was pillowed on the still-damp parachute roll, which was already rank with stale salt water.

She sat up. She couldn't see a rass. And it was so quiet! She remembered nights like this on dry land when the peeping of thousands of frogs would be deafening. No more frogs. Indicator species were dying out the world over.

There was a lightning flash, far out at sea. A few seconds later, a grumble of thunder. The storm. Was it coming this way? She hadn't made a shelter yet. And she had drunk untreated water. She resigned herself to the belly-griping that was sure to follow.

The quiet pressed in on her ears, insistent as a pressure wave. The darkness had its hands over her eyes.

Something rustled along the ground, a little way behind her. Jacquee swung to her knees and spun round. "Uncle?" she called out, her voice quavery. "Lickchop?" No answer.

She pulled her switchblade out of her front jeans pocket. At least she still had that. She snicked it open and held it low, near her thigh. She tried to calm her breathing so she could hear better. Finally she remembered she could see in the dark now, if she chose. If it was working. If she hadn't gone and infected her brain in her eagerness.

She breathed in. Then, slowly, out. She—is what Dr. Lin had called it? "Engaged her mindfulness." Then did the little twitch of lower eyelid, a half-wink, that should turn on the infrared. And gasped as the world blossomed into glowing blues and greens on a black velvet background. The rustling was coming from breadfruit tree leaves, big as dinner plates, that were being blown along the ground by the freshening breeze. The tree branched out above her. It was stunted, only about 15 feet high. But there were one or two green cannonballs of breadfruit amongst its branches. She hadn't even seen the tree when she made her way here in the daytime. Too feverish. Was it really there, or was she still delirious? No. Her head felt clear, and she was no longer shivering. The fugue seemed to be over.

There was a manicou on the tree's trunk, climbing higher. It was no bigger than Lickchop. It gripped a branch with its prehensile tail and turned to stare down at her. Its eyes glowed. It resumed its climb.

The tinkling sound of water drew her eyes to examine the place where she'd drunk from in her delirium. Not a river; a lagoon. Partly fed by the ocean. That's why the water was slightly salty. The water shifted back and forth. Her altered vision showed it black as tar, the plants around its edge a pale green.

Another mosquito bit her neck, and one whined in her ear. She looked down at her body. If she switched to heat signature

vision, she would be able to see her warmth that was attracting
them.

But first she had to make some shelter, since it seemed she
was going to spend the night there. Stringing the parachute
from a low branch of the breadfruit tree and digging a shallow
pit in the ground nearby for a solar still would have been easy
with her new mod, except her ankle sang with each step. By
the time she got set up for the night, she was sweating, drawing
mosquitoes in a cloud around her.

She couldn't bear the stinging any longer. Plus, she had to
wash the sea salt out of her clothes and put them to dry. And
relatively fresh water was right there, steps away. . . .

She promised herself she wouldn't drink any more of it, just
use it to clean herself and her clothes. Swim for a bit, escape the
mosquitos.

She removed her boots and socks, then stripped off the rest
of her clothing. The night air hardened her nipples. She limped
to the water's edge and eased herself in, shivering in the chillier
water. She trod water for a bit until she'd warmed up. Then she
took in a breath and let herself sink into the blue-green-black
world below.

When Jacquee was little, maybe eleven years old, and living
on land, she once had a homeroom teacher who'd made them
read a poem about some old-time Britishy town that slid into
a lake because the townspeople had been too stingy to give
bread to a starving beggar. She could be looking 'pon that town
now, settled down onto the lagoon bottom. Because there was
a nighttime city block down there. One quite a bit worse for
having been battered by the water. Rusted cars and lengths of
copper pipe. Broken bricks and chunks of cement. Waterlogged
tree trunks. Whole pieces of buildings, drowned for the world's

original sin; a human-triggered, human-stoked runaway train of climate change.

Moonlight beamed down through the water, making motes suspended within it twinkle: microorganisms; microplastics. The town was lit by fairy lights. Jacquee explored for a bit, wiping algae off street signs and peering in through slimy windows at sodden, broken computers and furniture, tossed every which way. Through one window she spied an armchair, upside down and semi-buoyant. She pulled away from that window quickly.

She dove down to street level. Tumbling through the diffuse beams were translucent blobs, rounded by wave action, each about the size of a soccer ball. They streamed along with the current. Filaments of blob-stuff, like tresses, trailed from them. She could see where in some cases, strands of filaments were caught in rock cracks, anchoring them. What the rass were those? She swam down toward the shimmering globules.

One of them had encased a whole shrimp; another, a small fish. She recoiled. Were they being digested? But no, both fish and shrimp were swimming calmly, going about their business. They didn't look engulfed. It was more as though they had sprung multiple antennae, all over their bodies.

Jacquee went up for air and dove back down a few times, trying to understand what she was seeing. The more she did, the more lagoon creatures she saw, apparently in symbiosis with the small clouds of who-knows-what. Phosphorescent, an oddly fuzzy turtle flippered lazily past her nose, seemingly unbothered by being coated with the strange organism. She spied three more.

All looked plump and healthy. Turtles were dying everywhere else, weakened by their softening shells.

Entranced, Jacquee dug a fist-sized lump of the matter out of a crevice in a rock. It was attached to the rock by a fleshy string. It looked as though swiping a finger through it would disperse it. But no; it was membranous, pale green with darker green filaments threaded through it. She rubbed it gently between thumb and middle finger. Slightly slippery. It didn't look or feel like a colony of tubifex worms, which is what she would have expected in a lagoon.

The blob began to glow more brightly, perhaps in response to her touch. The picky threads inside it began to undulate. Miniscule lightning-forks inside a tiny green cloud. She found herself smiling. The thing was beautiful. She brought it closer to her face to better inspect it.

Her action broke the umbilical connecting the blob to its rockstone. It convulsed and snapped toward her, flattening clammy against the side of her face and half-covering one eye. Jacquee clawed at it as she kicked for the air above. Her head broke the surface of the lagoon while she was still trying to scrape the thing off her face. It came away in strips, thin and flexible as skin. Fuck! Had she gotten all of it? She dunked her head back into the water and scrubbed her cheek and eye with one hand. Too late considered that it was the same hand with which she'd been holding the blob. She was probably just depositing more of it onto her face. She switched to the other hand and rubbed away all the remaining bits she could feel. She lifted her head for air again and kicked as quickly as she could for the edge of the lagoon. Once on land, she squatted and surgeon-washed her two hands in the water. Glowing motes flowed away from her hands, going dull again as she watched; remainders of the blob.

She put her clothes back on. They would dry more quickly against her skin. Then she sat at the waterside, knees clasped to her chest, and shuddered. Stupid. Stupid. To go and put her hands on some unknown organism.

With her night vision on, the retreating thunderhead was a light show. She watched the funnel of it move slowly away, lit up every few seconds by lightning flashes. She rocked and tried not to think of what would happen if no one found her. When the storm had disappeared over the horizon, she crawled into her shelter. She wadded her sweatshirt for a pillow. To keep the worst of the mosquitoes away, she cocooned herself in a trailing edge of the parachute. She turned her night vision off, leaving herself in the uncertain dark. Eventually, she sank into a slurry of disturbed sleep.

She woke ravenous the next morning. A sickly sunrise tinted the clouds with tainted orange-browns and greens, painterly and poisonous. Jacquee busied herself with the business of survival: drinking the cup of sterile water she'd gotten from the solar still; using her stick to knock a breadfruit out of the tree; the forever it took with two twigs and a guy line from the parachute to make a fire for roasting the breadfruit. While she ate, she tried to raise the ultralight's onboard computer with her addy. Only the crackle of static, which suddenly, alarmingly increased till it was like having ants crawling around inside her skull. She yelped, then mentally deactivated the addy.

Careful of her ankle, she slowly made her way a little higher up the elevation till she could see the beach where she'd come ashore. Or at least, where it had been. High tide had completely covered it, and the wreck of the ultralight was nowhere to be seen. The water had taken it, probably already swept it miles away out to sea.

Jacquee sat down hard on a rock. Things were bad. She had really messed up this time. How to let her taz know where she was? She didn't know how far away they were, or in what direction.

She scratched her forearm, and only then realized she'd been doing that all day. The forearm tingled, so gently she could have been imagining it. So did the side of her face. It was happening on the side of her body where the organism had tried to latch on to her.

Fuck, fuck, fuck. Jacquee tore up a handful of scrub grass and used that to scour her arm and face. All she got for the effort was dirt ground into the scrapes she was giving herself with the scrub grass; scrapes she wouldn't be able to wash clean until she'd collected more sterile water. That wouldn't be until next morning. And she needed to conserve the clean water for drinking, not bathing. The calculus of dampness, to rass. Jacquee swore and slammed her stick against the ground. She'd infected herself with a parasite, and she was injured. Her taz could probably fix both, but she was stranded with no way to contact them. She was fucked.

And if she wasn't careful, she was going to give herself sunburn into the bargain. She made her painful way back to the shade of the broad-leaved breadfruit tree. She sat morosely beneath it, pelting rockstones into the lagoon and cycling her vision through its different spectra. She was sweaty and lonely and her pig was gone. She wanted so badly to be where she usually went when she was in need of comfort; the water. She glared at the lagoon, lying there all spread out and tempting, making beckoning little wavelet sounds. She needed to survive, but for how long? Suppose rescue never came?

Survival. That's all she was doing. Survival and waiting. That's all the world was doing. Taz communities were self-sufficient and did better than much of the rest of humanity.

But really, they were doing the same as everyone else; making do with fewer and fewer natural resources as time went on. Treading water and praying in vain for rescue.

Did it have to go so?

Not quite sure what she was doing, Jacquee levered herself to her feet. She waded across the lagoon—because fuck it—to a patch of mangroves she'd noticed at the far side of its lip.

Seagulls wheeled and quarreled overhead as she swam. Her new vision showed her that the mangrove roots, where they entered the water, were as filamentous as any living thing in that water. And at first she thought the roots had somehow trapped rockstones between them, till a jolt of recognition told her what she was seeing. Oysters! In the wild! Her belly rumbled joyfully. She fell to her knees in the mud, dug out a bunch of them, and shucked them open right there-so. She looked at the glistening meat in the shells. She made her decision. She slurped down the oysters and their salty liquor, every last one.

Then she beat around the mangrove roots and the shore of the lagoon until she found another plastic bottle with no cracks in it. Blasted things were everywhere. She dove to the lagoon bed and collected a few of the smaller globules in her bottle. She returned to her campsite with it, and wedged the bottle upright in the mud near the water's edge to keep it cool. She had no idea what was going to become of her, but for now, her belly was full and her mind occupied. She crawled into her makeshift tent and dozed, dreaming big dreams. What would come, would come.

The sound of an air horn rousted Jacquee out from under the parachute. She looked out over the water. Three dots on the water, heading her way. Porkpies, or . . . ? She stayed up there, hidden by the trees, till she could see for sure. They were coming quickly. Pretty soon, she could make them out. Two electric speedboats. From her taz! She recognized the colorful patterns painted on their hulls. Kobe's on the left; green circuits painted on a black background. The red, green, and gold one on the right was Uncle Silvis's.

Jacquee's heart was slamming in her chest. She nearly sprained the other ankle hurrying down to the beach. She drew off her sweatshirt and waved it in the air. "Hey!" she shouted. "Over here!" The ocean breeze blew the sound off in another direction. Did they see her? Please. They had to see her.

They must have, because the boats started angling her way, bouncing through the swells. A small, black form clambered from inside Uncle Silvis's boat, plopped into the water, and started making for shore. Uncle Silvis had to stop and circle back. He plucked the wriggling body out of the water. Lickchop? Joy surged like storm seas. How was he alive?

Little more, the boats were close enough to shore that the two men were able to jump out onto the sand below the surface and begin pulling them out of the water. Jacquee waded to meet them, ignoring the ache of the waves yanking her injured ankle. Lickchop was out of the boat again, trotting to meet her. His coder was trumpeting, *Ja-kay!* over and over. Who the rass knew it could be so loud?

The men had their backs to her, concentrating on getting their boats safely out of the water. Kobe looked over his shoulder at her. He was grinning. Uncle Silvis never turned around. Uh-oh. She was in big trouble, and she knew it.

A low wave lifted Lickchop, bringing him to thump against her shin. Luckily, on her good leg. He was squealing and snorting, his snout turned comically upward to keep it out of the water. *Ja-kay!* said his 'coder. *Ja-kay good!*

Hanging on to her crutch for balance, Jacquee bent and one-handed, scooped the little pig's bristly, squirming body up into a hug. "Yes," she whispered against his shoulder, "I good." She blinked away the salt tears she was adding to the sea.

Lickchop was wriggling to get down. Kobe took him from Jacquee and lowered him into the ankle-deep water to splash happily around their feet. Jacquee supported herself with one hand on the gunwale of Kobe's boat as she followed them onto the beach. "How you find me?" she asked the two men.

Kobe replied, "We lost the signal from the ultralight. Thought you went down with it. Uncle Silvis was frantic. Everyone was."

Uncle Silvis only grunted and pulled his boat on ahead of Kobe's.

"But," Kobe continued, "we kept getting inteference on our channels; first one, then the next. And then the message came through clear; S.O.S. from Lickchop. Found him swimming in open water, belting out E.M. pulses to keep the sharks away. Bet you didn't know his head rig could do that."

She hadn't. "But how that helped you know where I was?"

Uncle Silvis, his boat now well clear of the water, was leaning against its side, arms folded, and scowling at Jacquee. "Rahtid little trenton kept saying him could hear you," he ground out. "We had to wait till low tide, but all the way here, that sintin on him head been calling out coordinates."

Maybe that explained the tickling between her ears, the ghost snippets of Lickchop's voice. That old Sean Paul song he loved. "Hmm. I think maybe I could hear him, too."

That got Kobe's attention. "Tell me more about that."

"Later. Uncle, I sorry about your ultralight. If you show me how, I will print out a replacement. You gwine haffe help me with the wiring, though."

Silvis's expression was unreadable. He rushed toward Jacquee and pulled her into his wiry, iron-cable arms. He smelled of sweat and ocean salt and good sensimilla. "Wha mek a pig be your salvation, ee Jacquee? A haram?"

Jacquee chuckled. "Promise I never going to put him on the supper table."

Uncle Silvis held her away at arm's length, a reluctant smile quirking his lips. "Never mind. Gwine treat the little so-and-so like a king from now on. He bring daughter Jacquee back to us. To me. You ready to come home?"

"Too ready. I haffe get some things first, though."

"Ee-hee? Like what?"

The parachute. They could mend it. And the bottle of lagoon water with the green globs in it. Jacquee smiled at Uncle Silvis. "I find something in a lagoon over there. A living thing. I think is new."

Uncle Silvis put an arm around her waist, started helping her limp in the direction she had pointed. Kobe and Lickchop followed. "A-whoa. And what you think it good for?"

"Me nah know. We should preserve a sample of it. Because I have an idea. Jamdown Ark, we could become a databank of gametes to reseed the waters with when the time come. Maybe we could even breed stronger strains. And then we could—"

Laughing, Kobe shook his head. "Lord Jesus, not another Jacquee idea for saving the world."

Uncle Silvis was smiling, though. "Tell it to me when we get back."

Lickchop butted the back of her calf. Second time he had avoided touching the injured leg. Jacquee wondered what the sensors that were apparently in his rig let him perceive. *Chow,* he said.

As Uncle Silvis's boat bounced on the swells, racing Kobe back to Jamdown Ark, Jacquee studied Lickchop. She asked him, for the first time, "Is what you are?"

Lickchop stopped rooting around under the gunwale to gaze 'pon her, his black-in-black eyes inscrutable. *Are pig mind,* his 'coder stated.

Is "pig mind" he was saying? Or "big mind"? Lickchop continued, *Is what Ja-kay are?*

Maybe "are" was the right word. Lickchop apparently knew what it was to be a neurolinked creature, after all. Maybe it didn't matter if the link was with an artificial network or an organic one. Maybe he was referring to her in the plural because like recognized like.

A seaweed-green tracery, barely visible under the skin of her forearm, had crept up toward her elbow. It itched. She couldn't be sure, but she suspected it was responsible for the interference patterns in her wetware display. They were almost beginning to make sense. The world was looking little bit different, in ways she couldn't yet articulate. She was changing. She should have been worried, but she wasn't.

She was cradling the bottle containing the lagoon creatures between her knees. She leaned over and with her free hand, scratched Lickchop under his chin. He grunted happily, angled his head so she could reach the best place. She echoed back his question: "What are I and I? We don't know, darling. Time will tell."

She leaned back to enjoy the salt spray the speedboat was kicking up onto her face as it hurried them home.

Clap Back

There was a time in my life where for various reasons, I was investigating so-called "Black Americana," which is a term sometimes used to describe older, kitschy home décor pieces caricaturing and mocking Black faces and Black life. In the story, I describe some of the popular images of the day. There are similar pieces deriding Indigenous, Latinx, Asian, and Middle Eastern people. I got such an odious crawful of this stuff that I knew an angry story was going to come out of it someday. This is that story.

2032

> "My brother is all the time putting soccer on TV when I want to watch tennis. I forgive him."
> —Embroidered square, Malawi group
> quilt project "The Forgiveness"

BURRI CREATES NEW LINE OF AFRICAN-INSPIRED KNITWEAR

LAST WEEK, designer Agnetta Burri introduced Forgetful, her new line of knitwear for the summer season. The
bold colours spill in splashes of geometric shapes that cling
unabashedly to the wearer's body, characterized by finger-
hiding sleeves and long trains on skirts, dresses, and pants
alike. In an interview given poolside at her Lake Geneva
chalet, the 27-year-old Swiss designer said, "I'm working
with 'The Forgiveness Project.' I'm sure you've heard of
it. A group of teenaged girls from a village in Madi, Mali,
something like that. They're making this huge knitted quilt
and working these, like, Arabic proverbs into the weave.
I think it's Arabic. And maybe it's prayers, not proverbs.
Well, I've contracted with them to create quilt squares for
display in my boutique. It's like, 'Forgive and Forget,' right?
They're writing some new stuff for me."

Burri, who has a degree in molecular biochemistry, was
originally the founder of a tech startup working on delivery methods for sending cancer-fighting agents to targeted
parts of the body. She moved on from that project into
the world of haute couture. She has used her biochemistry
background to develop a proprietary technique for im-
pregnating the fibers of each of her pieces with a story
that will temporarily soak into the wearer's skin. "No, you
won't be able to read it. Nothing will show on the skin or in
the fabric. You kind of absorb it, like those topical painkillers. And then the story just gets transported into the
body, and over the course of a few days, you'll be able

to recite the whole thing. You become a sort of megaphone for a story the world needs to hear. There are so many people whose stories don't get told, don't you think? I just want to do my part. And in a week's time the nanites dissolve; you, well, pass them out in your urine. Just these little nanobot stories in a compound with low molecular weight and a high water and lipid solubility. Those penetrate the skin the easiest. It's pretty safe. I've had it tested and certified. Everything's aboveboard."

When asked which stories will be woven into the pieces, Burri would not go into detail. "I must protect my sources," she said coyly. "I'd hate for anyone to take advantage of these innocent young girls."

Now that it's been unveiled at Paris Fashion Week, the Forgetful line will go into mass production. Burri says that the mass-produced pieces will not have stories embedded in them. "I mean, that wouldn't exactly be consensual, right? No, it's only the custom-made couture pieces from the collection that have them. Those are going to a handful of customers, and they've all signed consent forms. The artisans and models of my couture house, too."

"Interest on foreign-aid loan is too high. My country can never pay it off. God says usury is a sin. I forgive you."

—Attributed to "The Forgiveness Quilt," author anonymous

A hush had fallen in the gallery. It wasn't like there were a ton of visitors; it was only a student group exhibition, after all. But this was it for Wenda's class cohort. After this, the class of 2032 would be able to graduate. There would be no more of Wenda having to wrangle with her committee over whether Black protest art was "overinscribed." No more security guards mistaking her for an intruder when she was cleaning up the studio after TAing late-night classes. Her classmates would go on to do whatever they did. And Wenda would probably go to jail. But she'd have her fucking degree.

They were all watching her. Her friend Mèdouze caught her eye. He was standing next his own project, a video installation. Queer trans identity, colour theory, found objects. Right now, Wenda was so nervy that the details blurred in her mind, even though she'd helped him work on his artist's statement. Mèdouze made a heart-shaped gesture against his torso and blew her a kiss for encouragement. Wenda smiled shakily back at him.

Wenda's bones were lead. Her eyes had turned to sand. Last night was only the most recent of many all-nighters. She blew out tired air, trying not to fret about what Toulema might be writing about her.

She pulled on the crisscrossed flaps of the box closest to her. They popped open with a soft puff, filling her nose with dust mites and the smell of old things. She sneezed. She reached into the box for one of her finds and unwrapped the tissue paper protecting it to reveal a ceramic tobacco jar. The jar was in the shape of a man's head. He was middle brown. His expression was lascivious. His lips took up most of the bottom half of the jar. He had gold hoops in his ears. The jar's lid was in the shape of a turban. For the umpteenth time Wenda wondered: Was this really some nineteenth-century white guy's muddled notion of Blackness, or just his idea of kitsch?

She put the jar on the table and kept unboxing. The crowd began an uneasy murmur, leaning in closer to see better. Wenda unboxed the various Blackamoors attached to candlesticks, lamp bases, bookends. Serving, always serving. Stick pins in the likeness of little boys with skin literally black, also sporting the ubiquitous turban plus jeweled bell sleeves, puffy pantaloons, and slippers with upcurled toes. Ashtrays, always in pairs, in the shapes of men and women (always one of each), art deco sleek in pantaloons and little vests, sitting with their akimbo legs wrapped around the bowls meant for collecting cigarette ash. The women always with their nubbin breasts swinging open to the breeze. She'd found any number of brooches, vintage 1940s and 1950s, displaying the same dismissive uncertainty of aim (*"Madi, Mali, something like that . . ."*). The brooches depicted enameled vaguely Afro-Asiatic faces wearing improbable crowns. The Jemima figurines and cookie jars beamed their pleasure at being kitchen slaves. Mèdouze gasped audibly at those.

There was more: ashtrays in the form of constipated black toddlers sitting in outhouses, straining as they screamed, openmouthed (the open mouths were where the hot cigarette ash went). As ever, Wenda swallowed down the lump of hurt and betrayal that rose in her throat every time she saw this stuff. She could barely stand to touch it. She wished she could apologize to the pieces, contorted as they were into caricatures happy to serve, happy to entertain. No matter. This ended today. She was going to proclaim her truth, like the young African women knitting "The Forgiveness Quilt." People loved thinking that the quilt was an act of letting go of blame. Fuck that. Wenda knew different. Nah, those girls were naming the injustices they'd suffered for the world to see.

Worst were the reproductions. The same cornucopia of jocular racism, but newer, shinier, produced within Wenda's lifetime. It made her feel sick to touch them. But the more modern polymers from which they were molded were the easiest to inspirit. Her iwin would penetrate the resin, carrying a plasticizer that would soften the material into pliability.

She creaked to her feet, grimacing at the grinding of her knees. Around the edges of the table she ceremoniously laid all the joke ephemera: Valentine's Day cards, which depicted the "couple" as a cartoonishly uglified Black girl and boy in tattered clothing, the boy offering wilted wildflowers and the girl declaring through lips fat as hams a vaguely salacious delight in some white person's contemptuous rendition of Black speech; old postcards of little Black boys, their faces twisted in pain as geese snapped off the chubby penises they'd stuck through holes in wooden fence posts to take a leak.

The assortment of horrors was now fully on display. Wenda straightened and arched her back to ease its twinging. She would've cringed in shame if anyone but Mèdouze had seen how she'd been spending so much of her free time—and her scant teaching assistant's salary—trolling antique shops and internet auction sites to buy this crap. It would have looked to the outside eye like internalized racism of the obsessive-compulsive kind. She was calling the performance "Clap Back." Some aspects of it were as illegal as balls. Sometimes protest art just was; how you gonna change the world if you play within its rule set? She'd fudged the details with her committee; what they didn't know wouldn't hurt her. Besides, once they witnessed it in action, she hoped the final result would blow them away. If it worked. She only had one chance to get this right. If it flopped, all she'd have was a table piled with ugly shit.

INFLUENCER JODRI LAFITTE THE FIRST TO UTTER WORDS HIDDEN IN FORGETFUL COUTURE LINE

Mr. Jodri Lafitte, internet darling and makeup artist, today was the first to utter a "storylet" absorbed through his skin from a sweatshirt custom-made for him by designer Agnetta Burri's couture house. Mr. Lafitte recorded the whole event and uploaded it immediately to his image channel.

▶| click to view video

Speaking eerily in the voice of a young woman, Mr. Lafitte intoned:

> "A police came to our school and said if girls wear tight dresses, boys will molest us. I forgive him."

Then he giggled in surprise at the sounds coming from his mouth. Mr. Lafitte said the sensation of nanites being absorbed into the flesh of his forearm "tickled, like bubbles in champagne."

According to Burri, Mr. Lafitte will experience the compulsion to repeat the words six or seven times a day for a week before the nanites degrade and are flushed out safely in his urine. The sweatshirt is one of only seventeen pieces from Burri's new Forgetful line of clothing to be custom-made for a handful of select buyers. All seventeen pieces have a quotation embedded into a patch of their fabric's weave.

Wenda lifted the final items out of the last of the boxes: apron, mask, surgical gloves, paintbrush, and a tightly sealed jar. She donned the protective clothing, then held the jar up to the light. The clear liquid inside sloshed with the viscosity of slightly soapy water. To look at it, you would think it *was* water. Wenda'd been stashing it in her fridge. A couple of times, she'd absentmindedly been about to drink from it, till the smell—a combination of heavy fleshiness and ammonia—had alerted her. After that, she'd clearly labeled the jar "Iwin" and sealed it into a sandwich bag for good measure.

Iwin. That's what Wenda had dubbed the invisible sprites floating in her custom blend of plasticizers, amino acids, and dissolved glucose. The English word "ghost" didn't quite do it for her, so she'd gone with her dad's native Yoruba word. The world had other names for what the iwin were—micro this, pico that—but these were hers, obedient to her. So she'd named them, as any doting mama would.

What had eventually worked as a carrier was a strain of *Clostridium sporogenes* her poor cat Sable had picked up. The vet said he'd probably gotten cut or something while roaming around the fenced backyard. The infection had gotten into the bone. He'd looked as though he were rallying, so the vet had let Wenda take him home. But Sable died a few hours later. Wenda buried him in her landlady's backyard. She figured it was only justice that she enslave the nasty strain, put it to work as payback for Sable. With any luck, the iwin would infiltrate the bacteria, suppress the natural eucaryote behaviors, and replace them with the iwin's own programmed ones.

Thank heaven for that double major. Even so, the coding that had gone into the iwin had been a stone bitch. She'd found a code string on the Dark Web and blended it into one of her own, adding "wake" and "cease" prompts, and a trigger. Tricky, but she'd finally gotten it as close to right as she could tell. Stroke of luck, finding that string that the poster said had "fallen off a truck." It consisted of instructions for penetrating and altering dense substances—just what she'd needed.

With the paintbrush, Wenda carefully coated each of the horrid memorabilia with the liquid from the jar. People wrinkled their noses at the smell wafting up from the table: life and unlife in combination. As she worked, she quietly whispered over and over, breathing the words into the still-wet coating: *"Please make this work. Please make this work."* Maybe speaking her intention would help. It certainly couldn't hurt. Intention was plenty. It had brought the horrors on the table into existence, after all.

Done. She set her paintbrush down. Now she had to work quickly. Only a couple of minutes before the plasticizer penetrated the pieces.

She took down her heavy dreadlocs, silver-threaded after years of grad school. This part of the work was better done with unfettered hair. She pulled the whistle out of her apron pocket. She'd carved it from a thigh bone of Sable's. It was clumsily made, full of chipped-out places. Wenda hadn't known how to carve, so she'd followed an online tutorial on making a whistle out of dried bone. She'd given herself a bunch of accidental nicks. She discovered that rubbing the blood into the bone then polishing the surface gave the whistle a pleasing brown stain, like antiquing.

Heart thrumming, Wenda blew a breathy tune through the whistle. She'd designed those notes, those particular vibrations played in that order and that timbre, to activate the iwin. This was modern-day hoodoo. Time was, you'd have had to boil a black cat alive, not salvage from an already dead one.

Wenda clutched the whistle and waited. Seconds passed. Wenda bit the inside of her bottom lip nearly raw with the tension of it. Toulema watched judgingly, the inside corners of eyebrows squeezed together.

There came the faintest pulse, as though someone had patted the skin of the air like the surface of a drum. "Whoa," murmured one of the onlookers. A few people clapped their hands to their ears.

Wenda's scalp prickled. Toulema yelped. On the table, the memorabilia were beginning to move. The iwin had molded and jointed them, giving them insectoid, limb-like levers, their edges imperfectly aligned with other elements of the sculptures and drawings. A lamp glided around the tabletop on hairlike appendages scuttling beneath its base.

Wenda dimly knew she was hyperventilating. Her teeth were chattering out a tympanum of terrified exhilaration. In the fugue state brought on by accumulated years of worry and sleep deprivation, her vision doubled. She knew what she was seeing, but her mind's eye overlaid it with what she'd dreamed of: Turbans being unwound from sweating heads. Clay and enamel knuckles scrubbing relief into crinkled hair that had been trapped under the masking winding cloths for centuries. Black and brown fingers buttoning vests closed to cover nipple-less breasts, previously exposed. The constipated babies, their bellyful bowels loosened, shitting out flaming tobacco embers with explosions of sulfur, then running giggling away from their burning outhouse prisons to play with their friends. Lips relaxing from cooning rictus into genuine, full smiles and raucous laughter. Endless slices of watermelons being drop-kicked into the air to burst apart and rain down sweetness. Water bowls that had strained unreleased arms for hundreds of years being upended over their carriers' heads, waterfalling cleansing baths. Tattered clothing mending itself into a riot of defiant, contrary stylishness.

Wenda shouted with glee. It had worked. Her shoulders relaxed, more fully than she'd known possible. "No more," she told her poppets. She raised her voice so the stunned gallery could hear her: "No more being frozen in attitudes of submission, no more fetching and carrying. No more smoking ash tipped through your lips into your screaming baby bellies. Kill those fucking penis-nipping geese and roast them for a party. A fucking party, y'hear? No more pick-a-nigs. You're retired."

Her poppets slid down the table legs and followed her as she marched to the gallery's front door and opened it for them. The New Black streamed through, out into the unsuspecting world. Wenda stayed behind to face her audience.

The attendees glanced uncertainly at each other. Then Mèdouze began clapping. Hesitantly, the rest joined in. Toulema's brows had ascended into the stratosphere. In the semaphore of Toulema, you never knew whether that was good or bad. But at least she'd put her damning notebook away.

Wenda was too jittery with reaction to know what she felt. It wasn't over. No one had asked her yet what the iwin-driven poppets were going to do out in the world. For now, she would have a glass of the cheap red wine at the bar, chat with Mèdouze for a bit, then stagger home and collapse into bed.

Rap star Songtesta has announced her intention to reveal her Forgetful phrases at a pop-up private party on her yacht in the very near future. She's carefully timing when she will first don her Forgetful garment, an elaborately deconstruct-ed ball gown with its seams visible, so that her storylet will be in her bloodstream during the event.

Although none of the mass-produced versions of the For-getful line contain the surprise storylets, they do have a select number of "The Forgiveness Quilt" sentences screen-printed onto them. Within twenty-four hours of Mr. Lafitte's unveil-ing, department store sales of the clothing skyrocketed five hundred percent.

"Auntie gave me gravy with peanuts in it. I nearly died. I forgive her."
—Malawi group project, "The Forgiveness Quilt"

By the time Wenda dragged herself from sleep the next day, the gallery manager and Toulema had between them left seven messages in her voicemail. She texted them both to tell them she'd be at the gallery in an hour. When she got there, the manager was jigging around just inside the front door, waiting for her. He said, "Can you tell me just what's going on here, Wenda?"

Wenda approached her project table. What she saw made her clap her hands in glee. The table was twice as full of manikins as it had been the day before. Having no further orders programmed into them, they milled around restlessly. But each of the original ones had done its job—raided the city's antique and thrift stores, found another atrocity similar to itself, and touched it, imbuing it with iwin as well. Then they'd all come back here.

Wenda used her cell phone to videotape documentation showing that there were now more poppets than before. The manager's questions became more strident. She handed him her cell phone. "Would you record this next bit for me?" she asked. "No sound, though." Wouldn't do to have anyone be able to copy the tune.

She stood in front of the table and played the "subside" notes. The manikins went still. Wenda ached to see their unlife taken away from them. Just memorabilia, she reminded herself. Not the real thing. She took her phone back from the manager and thanked him. "They're deactivated now," she told him. "Permanently."

Then she caught a bus to campus. Term wasn't over yet. She had a discussion to lead that afternoon. Still needed that paycheck, after all.

"Twelve hours working every day in running shoe factory. I have twelve years old. I forgive you."

—From the Malawi "Forgiveness Quilt," author anonymous

COUTURIER AGNETTA BURRI ARRESTED

Oh my darlings, how the pricey have fallen! Hold on for the ride; this scandal's going to be a bumpy one.

Last year, we couldn't get enough of tech-startup-whiz-kid-turned-designer Agnetta Burri's Forgetful clothing line. We fell over ourselves in the department stores to pay a good portion of a month's wages for "destructed" fashion that looked as though it'd been through a trash compactor then vomited on by a toddler who'd eaten too many Skittles.

But expensive as the ready-to-wear version of the line was, customized pieces cost a pretty penny more. The seventeen wealthy or famous enough souls who snapped these pieces up received a little something extra woven right into the fabric: invisible micro-robots that sank into the wearer's skin like shea butter, causing the wearers to randomly recite snappy little phrases from the Malawi "Forgiveness Quilt" project for a week. More about the quilt project later.

After seven days of using their owners as their mouthpieces, the wee robots would deactivate, break down into their component parts, and be flushed harmlessly out of the body. I'm sure you can guess how. Does it all sound just a bit . . . science fiction-y, my dears? Of course it does. The future is here, and we must come to terms with it.

There's a catch, though; turns out there's a glitch in the programming. The tiny micro-nanites don't deactivate or break down before exiting their hosts and being flushed into our sewage systems. In fact, scientists are fearing that some of them may be replicating themselves. The problem was first detected when doctors began reporting on rare but mysterious cases of people developing short-lived urges to quote words of wisdom from the Freedom Quilt project. (For me, the real horror is imagining how the nanites are getting from our sewers into other people's bodies. And now I bet you're imagining it too, aren't you? Good. I shouldn't have to bear this burden alone.)

It turns out that La Burri isn't the hotshot programmer she told us she was. In fact, she didn't do the work at all. She put a team of coders together, then snatched their work from them before it was finished, because she wanted to have the Forgetful clothing line ready in time for the Paris season.

And "The Forgiveness," my darlings? That heart-warming meme about a group of young African girls using the power of knitting to forgive us all our sins? An utter fabrication, invented by Agnetta Burri to boost her sales! She took a chance on the tried-and-true technique of marrying fashion with light blackface, and as ever, scads of us found it irresistible. Burri didn't even write the homilies herself! That was uncredited wordsmithing by the artisans who toil in her couture outfit, custom-fitting every dart, pleat, and cunningly shaped French seam.

Overnight, Agnetta Burri has gone from *Forbes* woman of the year and youngest self-made billionaire to pariah. *Forbes* has revised its estimate of her net worth to zero, and *Fortune Magazine* just declared her one of the "World's Most Disappointing Leaders." Her trial is set for later this year.

In the meantime, my lovelies, if you find yourself mysteriously quoting the words of an overworked sequin setter in a Paris design house, don't worry. It'll pass in a week or so. It's happening to more and more people nowadays. In fact, it's all the rage.

> "Tourists come to see our dolphins. They leave trash
> that kills the dolphins. Do the dolphins forgive them?"
> —From Burri hoax "The Forgiveness Quilt"

Wenda was surprised to see who her visitor was. Usually it was family coming to see her. Even though the charge had only been petty theft, the judge had decided to make an example of her Black ass. A ten-year sentence for making away with a handful of tchotchkes. Whereas this chick had thrown money at her even bigger problem, paid a few million in damages, and had never done a day of jail time. Wenda breathed down the bitter. She knew the way of the world. Had getting herself put in here made even a bit of difference?

She sat at the long table. In a line on either side of her, other inmates were holding conversations with visitors through the plexiglass barrier. There was laughter, tears, shouting: the usual. She picked the phone up and stared at the chicly understated woman sitting across from her. "Ms. Burri," Wenda said, "what can I do for you?"

To Wenda's surprise, Agnetta Burri's eyes were glistening with tears. "How did you do it?" she said. "How did you get them to come back? How did you turn them off?"

Idiot of a woman. Had other people do her work for her and couldn't even get that right. Her tech team had quit, had black-listed her in the industry, and she couldn't figure out how to undo her own mistake. Wenda replied, "I'll tell you how. You'll have to visit my friend for part of it. He graduated in my same year. But I'll need you to do two things for me."

"So yeah," said Mèdouze's tinny voice over the phone. "No-body knows who did it, but our whole graduating year had their student loans completely paid off! Undergrad, grad, every discipline, every major! Isn't that wild?"

"Really?" said Wenda. "Everyone?"

"Mm-hmm."

"Even me too, I guess. I should get my mom to check." That'd be handy, to get out of prison with no school debt.

Mèdouze said, "You don't sound surprised."

"It's hard to surprise me anymore. Listen, my phone time is almost up."

"Right. Hey, some woman called. She wants that creepy whistle of yours."

Huh. Agnetta was really going to try it. "I know who she is. Give it to her. Pretty sure she'll get it back to you." The guard was coming her way. "Gotta go, honey. Love you."

"Love you, too."

Three days later, puzzled emptiness was echoing through the "Black Memorabilia" sections of the online auction platforms, at least for a moment; for a few blessed hours, there were no listings for "Cute Little Negro Boy Figurines" or "Black Americana." Vintage shops were reporting thefts, though some people swore they'd watched the collectibles march out of the stores under their own steam. Agnetta Burri was keeping her second promise.

2082

> "My parents are making me marry a man five
> times my age. Someday, I may forgive them."
> —Phrase in the style of "The Freedom Quilt"
> coined by a rogue nanite

In the middle of the night, Xiomara's phone rang, waking her up.

Why wasn't Perry in bed beside her?

The phone kept ringing. Scared now, she answered it. Her heart started slamming in her chest. She said, "I'll be right there, Officer."

It was nearly 2:30 a.m. by the time she got herself and Perry safely back home. Xiomara put her purse on the living room table. "Come, sit," she said to Perry. She took him by the hand and led him to the couch, but he just stood there in front of it. His face was drawn. So she said, "Let me tell you a story." Six years married, and they still played this game with each other.

He gave her a quizzical look; her timing was odd, and she knew it. But he lay on the couch. He had to bend his knees in order to fit. He put his head in her lap. He was trembling. So was she. She took three fibrillating breaths to collect her thoughts and began. "There once was a woman who collected ghosts." Now, where in the world had that come from? Oh, right. Her grandmother and her precious iwin. Xiomara hadn't thought about that story in years.

"Was she a sister?" Perry's voice shook. "The ghost collector?"

"Yes, a sister. Beautifully Black as a moonless night, with one hell of a 'fro. Like Angela Davis in the seventies big. No, twice as big. A 'fro high as mountains."

"Old-school woman, then."

"The oldest. And curves like L.A. freeways."

"Yes, Lord." His body had relaxed a little against her thighs.

Xiomara snapped her fingers to get the house's attention. She conjured up a drawing pad. The transparent rectangle hung in the air, outlined in green light. She tapped the screen to get the haptics going, selected a clean pencil line of deep, warm brown. A few strokes with her index finger to outline the suggestion of a face, sturdy nose, chewy lips. Lines of experience deepening the face's beauty. A calm resolve in the eyes. Sure, that could be Nan-Nan as Xiomara remembered her.

"And in that hair," Xiomara said, "was where she kept the ghosts."

Perry's eyes were closed, as though he were drifting off to sleep. After a few seconds, he muttered, "What kinds of ghosts in her hair?"

"What kinds do you want?"

"Happy ones."

She shook her head. "No Caspers. Not in my story. Think again."

He considered for a second. He sat up and leaned over her lap so he too could draw on the screen. "Ghosts of the should," he said. He used his index finger to tap all around the woman's head. "Ghosts of the will. Hoodoo spirits, their hearts overflowing with centuries of rage. H'ants holding their torn-out eyes in their hands, yet still bearing witness. Duppies and jumbies, and their jamboree is a revolution." He kept going until Nan-Nan was adorned with a halo of hair. And still he kept tapping at the screen till he was jabbing, stabbing with those fingers and the screen was flashing REDUCE FORCE, REDUCE FORCE.

Xiomara reached out and covered his hand with both of hers. Not that she could do so completely; those big hands were two of the many things she loved about her man. He curled his fingers into his palm and himself into her embrace. He was shaking again. She rocked him as best she could. He tilted his head back, letting her shoulder support it. His eyes were shut. After a time, he gave a shuddery sigh. Opened his eyes to stare at the ceiling. Low, he muttered, "I didn't do anything wrong."

"Don't give them any reason to notice you. None."

"I didn't!"

"Did you put the renewal sticker on your license plate, like I told you?"

"Two days ago."

"Did they think you were someone else?"

He kept staring up into the white nothing of the ceiling above them. "No. They stopped me because they felt like it." He bit his lips. "They impounded my car. But first they tore the seats apart. Tore them to shreds. Foam and cotton everywhere. I asked them what they were looking for. That's when they slammed me down over the hood. One of them put his gun right in my face."

Her stomach leaped up into her throat. "Perry, they could have killed you!"

"Let it go, Xiomara. Yes, they stopped me. Yes, they pulled their guns on me even though I had both hands in the air and they could clearly see I was unarmed. They wrenched my shoulder good; I could hear the joint creaking—"

A single sob burst from Xiomara's lips.

"—but they didn't shoot me. I'm not dead. I'm not the statistic this time."

"This time."

"Yeah, this time! In this world, in this country, that's the best I can do!"

"It isn't good enough!"

They were both breathing hard. Her arms around him had tightened into steel. He winced, trying to shift his shoulder. Xiomara relaxed her grip. Got her breathing under control. "I'm sorry, lover. I'm just glad you're home."

He didn't answer. She tried again: "Can I get you an ice pack for your shoulder?"

He started shivering again. "No ice pack," he said through

chattering teeth. "A couple of ibuprofen would be nice. And some mint tea."

"That's it? You sure?"

"Yeah. I'll take tomorrow off, go to the doctor first thing."

In the kitchen, Xiomara used the whistling of the kettle of boiling water to hide the sound of her racking sobs. Then she washed her face and took Perry his tea and the meds.

They went to bed. Eventually, Perry fell asleep, but Xiomara couldn't. *Ghosts of the should,* he'd said. *Ghosts of the will.*

Xiomara sat straight up in bed. She'd just had the most outrageous idea. *I mean, who would do something like that? Who would even consider it?*

But the notion wouldn't go away, so consider it she must. It was a terrible idea. She eased herself out of bed and went to the living room. She animated the drawing of the woman she and Perry had done together, giving it three dimensions. It did look a bit like her long-gone Nan-Nan. Xiomara hadn't spoken with Wenda's memory bank in years. Wenda'd been a badass. They put her in prison, but she went and found herself the best girlfriend ever in there. And when they were both finally out, they went and found themselves another. Together, the three of them had revived Agnetta Burri's failed tech startup, the one from before Burri's ill-fated designer exploits, and turned it into what it'd set out to be in the first place.

Xiomara turned the image on the screen into an icon, linked it to her grandmother's avatar, and called Wenda up.

The avatar's eyes brightened in recognition. It smiled at her with Nan-Nan's mischievous grin. "Hey, Xiomara."

"Hey, Nan-Nan. It's good to hear your voice."

"What's up, sweetie? You look as though you have something on your mind."

Xiomara chuckled. Alive or dead, Nan-Nan could always tell. Her memory bank was a far cry from sentient. But it could be uncanny. She remembered that from just after Nan-Nan died. In her grief, Xiomara would talk to Nan-Nan's avatar for hours every night, until one night it told her out of the blue that her friends were probably missing her, and she should start hanging out with them again.

Xiomara said, "I just need someone to talk to. Perry's asleep right now. Nan-Nan, there are still wild micro-nanites out there from that crazy designer lady, right?"

"Yeah. They didn't all come back to her. At least she managed to switch off their ability to replicate, and that was good enough. The few remaining ones will degrade eventually."

"I could turn it back on, though. The replication."

Nan-Nan smiled. "I know you could. You take after your grandma." Then Nan-Nan's eyes went wide, a convincing imitation of life. "But you aren't serious, are you? Why would you want to do that?"

"First I'd have to reprogram them. Make them able to alter gene markers for race."

She told Nan-Nan her idea. When she was done, the AI busted out laughing, so loud that Xiomara had to turn the sound down so as not to wake Perry. "You want to make everyone Black!"

"Maybe? But, Nan-Nan, here's what I'm trying to figure out. Whiteness already tries to take everything they want from Blackness. Must they have our skins, too? What evidence would be left of our authentic selves?" As she spoke, Xiomara brought the avatar's hair to life with ghost after angry, howling ghost. *Ghosts that had been enslaved.* "And what about everyone else's identities? There are more than just white and Black people in the world." She packed more and more ghosts into the image's hair. *Ghosts that had had a dream.*

Nan-Nan smiled. Quietly, she said, "Those already paranoid people who are convinced that whiteness is being bred out of existence would really lose their shit."

Xiomara chuckled. "Yeah."

"Darling, do you still have the whistle?"

"Yes, Nan-Nan." It was one of her most prized possessions.

"Well, your name does mean 'battle-ready,' after all. If you decide to do this, I'll teach you the two tunes: start code and kill code."

"You'd do that for me?"

"Of course, my lovely. It's all up to you. Just say the word."

Xiomara thanked the memory bank and dismissed it. That left only the avatar on the screen. Xiomara stared at it for a long minute. The Nan-Nan that Xiomara knew had had a big 'fro, but she'd seen pics of a younger Nan-Nan, with fat, bouncy dreadlocks down to her hips.

Xiomara began to work on the image again. She cloned the ghosts that made up its hair until the hair separated into sections and lengthened into thick black coils hanging down past its shoulders, each coil a tangled mass, strong and toothy as barbed wire, of striving and fighting and dying and loving and laughing and birthing and singing and worshipping and being uppity or cowed or jubilant or sad and fighting fighting fighting and never giving up. *Ghosts that had led their people to freedom.*

Ain't we people, too? she thought. *Wouldn't freeing us be a step toward freeing all humanity? Would dark skin cease to be an axis of violence if everyone had it?*

Did she dare? She sat in the dark, trying to decide.

On the screen, ancestor Wenda shakes her head as though to music, the fat, eager coils of her hair slapping across her face as she does. Her iwin flap free, keening scraps of grey that skirl and twirl until they've whipped her locs up into a silver cloud cyclone.

The ghost with ghosts in her hair stills. She gives Xiomara a mischievous grin and calmly waits for her decision.

    Yet where can we go that they will truly know us?
    Into our heads, if we're lucky,
    If we're lucky, into our lovers' arms.

Pocket Universe

*This is another commissioned story written in response
to an artwork. (Could that be considered ekphrasis? I'm
still grappling with the meaning of the term.) "Rehous-
ing" by Peter Friedl is "a series of works by Peter Friedl
which comprises a selection of individual, intricate, and
true-to-scale models of houses." "Pocket Universe" is a
very short story, a flash piece about a woman at the end
of her life, imagining her final home. Short, but I packed
a lot of associations and ideas into it. I won't name them
all here. I'm not trying to write spoilers with these notes.
But which ones will you spot? More importantly, what
associations and ideas does the story convey to you? A
story is a mirror. What do you see?*

SADIKA GRIMACED as the artist caseworker fitted the visor over
her head. They'd swabbed the rubber seal with alcohol after
the last person used it, but the alcohol was still wet and warm
as sweat. It had soaked into the worn rubber. The visor sealed
against her face with a squelch.

"Comfy?" the artist asked. Alistair, he said his name was. Trim, ageless Black man, managed to make his hospital whites and matching tennis shoes look dapper. His voice came conducted through the bones in her ears, eerily both intimate and distant. He didn't wait for Sadika to reply. "Okay: sight, smell, touch, hearing, or taste?"

Sadika relaxed gingerly against the couch's cushions, wincing against anticipated pain. Painkillers hadn't quite kicked in yet. Doctors said the soreness in her back was because her lungs were now affected. "Affected." Such a neutral word for what was really going on in her body.

But the movement hurt less than she'd expected. The couch cradled her without compressing any part of her. "Just bury me in this then, nuh?" she joked. "I feel like I lying in angel wings and cotton puffs."

Alistair chuckled. "Be amazed how many patients ask that. All right. Pick one of your five senses, please."

Sadika sighed, the movement of her inhalation bringing a dull echo of an internal elbow to the ribs. She considered for a few seconds. "Taste."

She'd thought she would feel something from the sensors all over her scalp, suckered onto her poor bald scalp like leeches. Instead, her mouth sprang water as it filled with the starchy, liquid pleasure that was Maami's red peas soup. "Mi lawd!" she exclaimed, and automatically held her hands to her mouth to catch the liquid she was sure would spill from it. But of course there was nothing there.

Alistair's amused voice in her ear said, "Don't worry. No food not really in your mouth."

But it might as well have been. Sadika let the soup taste dance over her tongue. Salty, like her grandmother had liked it. Maami's pressure was what had killed her, but she'd always eaten just what she wanted. Said life was too short to deny herself.

But the sensation in her mouth was too cold, though, and too slimy. Sadika wasn't sure what her brain did to communicate that to the interface, but in a few seconds, it was just right. Warm and something else. Unguent; that was the word. Then the conviction she was tasting soup faded entirely.

Alistair said, "Sorry about that. I had the gain up too high, and you got some feedback. But I can use what I got. Pick another sensation, please, Miss Lawton."

"I could pick taste again? Or it have to be something else?"

"Up to you. You don't have to do anything in order. Is your resting place, after all. You just tell me what you want."

"That's the problem. I don't know what I want."

"Tell me what you're most proud of in your life."

"Who, me? What somebody like me have to be proud of, or not be proud of? I get born, I lived, and now I dying. When I gone, my ashes going to rest in the burial house you making me. So just make me a house then, nuh?"

"Yes, but the house have to come from you. It have to sum up your life, come from your imagination. Try touch. What memories you get from that?"

Sadika focused on the bulbs of her fingertips, on what they made her think of. "I guess I'm supposed to be thinking about the feel of my babies' skins soft under my hands, or of a lover."

Alistair smiled, his features lit by the glow from the monitor. "If you want. Though in my line of work, we call that a cliché."

Sadika chuckled. "I see." In any case, the sensation making her fingers tingle wasn't the expected. It was a smooth, metallic, moveable. And a pulling feeling that went a little way up her arm, accompanied by a click.

"What is that?" Alistair asked.

"Car doors. The handles."

"Huh. Different cars?"

"Yeah. Passenger sides, mostly. I used to work the stroll, you know. When I was young. The one down on the east side. I got into plenty plenty cars."

"Me, too," Alistair replied. "Started there as a poor young artist. I didn't like all those different people touching me all the time, but some of them were nice. I decided I liked the comfort work business, so now I do this." He fiddled with his screen. Its back was to her.

Sadika grunted. "I never thought too much about liking it or hating it. It was a job. I was good at it, is all."

"So why you want to make it part of your coffin memorial?"

Sadika let the sense-memory from her fingertips extend all the way through her body. The cramped spaces in all those cars, the tiny universe each one had created, stretched to bursting to hold two people for a short space of time. The sliding of slick, damp flesh against and in hers. The comforting smell of warm skin and latex. The muscle-fatigued ache in her jaw and her nethers after a busy night. The shudders and moans she elicited. Not always quiet. No two people came exactly the same way. She'd never lost interest in that. She was proud of the work she'd done.

She began to try to put it all into words for Alistair, but he shook his head and smiled. "Just think about it all," he said. "The sensors can tell which centres of your brain are lighting up."

He busied himself for a few minutes. "What else you want me to add in?" he asked.

The little bit of effort she'd expended on this had exhausted her. Irritably, she snapped, "Don't you have enough already?"

His reply was mild. "I do. Lie there and rest while the maquette rendering."

Now she felt bad for taking it out on him. Trying to make up for it, she said, "But you have people waiting, don't it?"

"Don't worry out your soul case. You rest little bit."

Alistair traced on the touch screen of his laptop, made mysterious gestures in the air. Sadika kind of wished she could see what he was doing, but he'd show it to her soon enough. Her mind drifted. She drifted a lot nowadays. All those powerful painkillers.

After more minutes than she'd kept track of, Alistair murmured, "Keep your eyes closed, Miss Sadika. I going to unhook you from this contraption. Then open your eyes slowly."

She didn't. She wanted to see what her memory had made. But her eyes opened onto darkness. Alistair had turned off the lights. She savored the dark, enclosed space. Just the two of them. For a short time longer.

Alistair said, "I going to on the light slow. Take time to get used to it."

"Chuh, man." Sadika didn't have time. Days, maybe. Weeks if she was lucky. Or unlucky. Truth to tell, Sadika was tired, to rass. Tired to her bones. This sickness wasted muscle, stole breath, made you a baby again. She struggled to sit up, clenched her teeth so as not to complain about Alistair's gentle hands helping her up. He plumped pillows behind her back while she strained to see the form on the screen he had turned toward her.

Smooth and bumpy. Round like bowls full of red peas soup, but made up of angles, all kinda different angles. Plenty plenty colours. Shaped by all those car doors into two joined domes, fat like bubbies, and, like hers, two slightly different sizes. The cancer had started in her left one. It pleased Sadika to think that her dead house would call her breasts to mind, for those who had eyes to see. Those breasts had fed her babies, had been suckled on by eager johns and lovers. Had given her and others pleasure.

She straightened up little more, to better see the maquette. No, it had three lobes, not two. Three, two; didn't matter. She used to have two breasts. Now she had one whole one and two scarred bumps, the keloided remainders of the other one. And pretty soon, she would be dust, and would have no bubbies at all.

"No handles on the doors?" she asked Alistair.

"You didn't imagine handles."

"Probably because I won't be getting out these doors."

He nodded. "A-true. You like it?"

"How big it going to be?"

"Big enough to hold your ashes. I think I will get car doors from the junk yard. Cut them in pieces. Weld them into the shape you see here."

"How long?"

"Maybe a week. You think you can hang on that long?"

She laughed. It hurt. "I will try. If not, them can just put me on ice till my new house ready for me."

Inselberg

Here is another piece centred around the fallout of precipitous ocean-level rise. With this one I just followed my nose, and it took me to some very weird places.

An inselberg is an abrupt outcropping of rock, geologically distinct from the surrounding area. An inselberg can also be home to flora and fauna only found on it. I'm using the word more metaphorically than scientifically for the island I've invented here. And whaddya know, there's another pig. Not in the least fluffy and cute, though.

> *Yam, feed me now.*
> *Yam, when I am dead,*
> *I shall feed you.*
> —a Nigerian grace

EVERYBODY GATHER ROUND the bus, now! Thank you please. Sir, beg you, don't try to pick the trumpet flowers. You might cause damage. Yes, sir; me know say you paid for an all-inclusive tropical vacation here on the little nipple of mountaintop that is all left of my country, but trust me. Some things you don't want all-included. Not since the sea uprise and change everything. Things like trumpet-flower bushes.

How many of you coming on the wondrous, watery tour? Gather in, everybody, so I could count heads. You in for a treat this morning, mek I tell you. Submerged cities, underwater skyscrapers, and an audience with the Wise Old Fish of the Mountaintop. If you ask him nice, maybe 'im will let us come back down from the peak. But be polite, you hear me? The tour last week had some from foreign ladies who feel say they were too tourist to mind them manners when tendering the requisite offering to the Wise Old Fish of the Mountaintop.

Sir, what you carrying on like that for? Didn't I tell you not to pick the trumpet-flowers? Stop with all the screaming, please. I warned you you might cause damage. Is all right, though. The trumpet flower plant is fair-minded. Even though you kill two of her future possible generations, she only take from you the same number of orchids you take from her. What, you didn't realize that "orchid" is Latin for "testicles"? Chuh. Just give thanks is only two flowers you pick. I don't know what woulda happen if you had pick three, or four.

Try and lie still, sir. Our friendly resort staff soon come and fix you up good-good. Just remember, gratuities not included in your bill. Our workers rely on your extra generosity as a reward for their good service, ascording to how seeing to your needs is the only industry ya-so nowadays. Here; you can use my scarf to stanch the bleeding. You don't want the smell of blood to bring the mongooses out from their holes.

But stop; the rest of oonuh not on the bus yet? Get on, get on! Can't keep the Perspicacious Mister Fish waiting! Yes, find yourselves a seat. We provide every luxury on dis-ya bus. We oxygenate and filter the air for your comfort, no extra charge. You can even take off your helmets; no airborne irritants in here! In your seat pockets, you will find your inflatables. You each get seven hundred. Don't fret; they indexed to the American dollar. In case of sudden tropical depression, you will find they remain relatively stable. Can't promise the same about Mister Fish, though!

Now, before we can set out on today's marvelous and malleable tour of our once-prosperous nation, oonuh haffee tell me if the password change.

Well?

No, lady, is not game me playing. What? You think I already know the password, only I not saying? But seeyah! After is you people from foreign who come up with the new passwords! You know, a code phrase you always want us to say to you at irregular intervals? Time was, it was "Yahman." No? Is the same one? Yahman, then; yahman.

All right, driver. We ready.

Guests of this beautiful resort, don't mind the lurching of the bus. This is one of the ones that wake up one morning with legs instead of wheels. Even the bus-them and all had to come to them senses and swim for dear life when that last duppy tide come through! Never mind, though. Here in the islands—or the mountains—we could do worse than have sentient buses. Biggest problem is when them take it into them head to hold our pickney-them to ransom in order to get more fuel.

Pickney? That mean child.

No, Ma'am; is no problem that you bring your nine-year-old on the trip with us. It will be educational for her, yahman.

By the way; if anybody see a pig deh-bout while we following the camino, him name Malky. If you see him, call him for me, do. Thank you please.

Over on your left, you can see the trembling waters of the island's former nuclear plant. You know what they say: "If my swamp a-rock, you best don't knock."

Mister, I mean don't get it into your head to go for no sea bath over there. You might come out again as pretty as me. You think I didn't notice you staring at me? If you tell me your room number, you and me could spend a little sweetness later. Ten percent surcharge, of course, and you haffe provide certification you had three clean blood tests in the past six months.

The extra eyes give me 360-degree vision, and at least me never have to worry with combing my hair anymore. To tell the truth, I think I was happy to lose it all and get more vision instead. Papa Fish tell me I must count my blessings.

If you cast your gaze just beyond the shivering bay . . . see that scrim on the other side of it? Forming what look like an edging between the mountain and the sea? Yes, Sir; like a frill. Well, that frill stretch all the way around the foot of the whole mountain, except for the places where the cruise ships dock at the resorts. You can guess what that frill is? Any of you ever read a book name *The Goats Look Up*? No, my mistake; *Stand on Zanzibar*. Ask not for whom the bell tolleth. That's all me a-say.

The bridge we crossing on right now is taking us over some famous ruins of former industry. This new body of water, we call it Sugar Lake. No, you can't get out the bus to take pictures. I know it smell nice, like boiled sugar sweeties. Funny thing about that duppy tide; time was, the biggest you would get is a king tide, and that was plenty big. All that melted ice from way up and down yonder.

Hey you, little nine-year-old pickney; you could tell me some of the effects of rising seas, of swollen oceans pushing an island like this one down under the sea? You look like a smart girl who pay mind to her lessons.

Yes, floods. What else? Rivers running backward, sewage rising up into the water table, crops deading because the soil get salinated. Very good! You forget one, though. For a long time, we didn't have beaches no more. People like you and your mummy stopped visiting us. Things did bad them there days. Not enough jobs, food crops doing poorly. But is all right; oonuh coming back again, both the tourists and the things that drowned. Why? Nuh this-yah duppy tide, this new thing? Nowadays, is like nothing that get drowned is really gone.

Duppy? How you mean, what it mean? Now that I think about it, oonuh been worrying out my soul case from the beginning, asking me what words mean. Aha. I see most of you never drink your phrasebooks this morning. You have to take a dose every day, for your protection. The water here not safe for oonuh to drink. You don't have resistance built up.

But I was saying: when the long time ago sugar plantations get submerge, is like that event leave a residue. A big sugar plantation duppy. It just sit down there below and a-brood. It make of every plantation the island ever had. All of them. All those boiling houses where people who look like me—but with fewer eyes—were forced to feed long poles of sugar cane they had cut from the fields into the grinders, to squeeze out the sweet juice. Then they had to pour the juice into some rahtid big cauldrons to render it down to molasses, and then to sugar. Every so often, one of the people who looked like me (except; eyes) would nod off from fatigue and get a hand caught in a grinder. So all those duppy hands, they sitting down below, too.

Beg pardon, Ma'am. I don't mean to upset your little girl, after she so clever. But I have this tour guide script to follow, you see? Koo here, see how the script get tattooed on the inside of my bottom lip, in peeny little letters? The whole script fix deh-yah in my mouth, so you understand I don't have no choice but to speak it. Is Master Fish make it to be so, yahman.

I could continue? Thank you please.

Oonuh sure you don't spy a pig out there in the murk? I hope he not lost. He's such a little guy, only standing as high as my shoulder. I prefer to have him with us on these rides. He help to keep the mongooses away.

Long and short of it is, that swamp below make of molten sugar. True we call it Sugar Lake, but is more like Syrup Swamp. Now we have to move along. If the bus stop here too long, the heat of the bridge will burn her poor feet. The pain give her the belly runnings, and we inside that self-same belly at the moment.

The facilities? Absolutely, sir. The water reclamation unit is at the back of the bus. Any other bodily fluids you care to donate while you in there are gratefully appreciated. Or any bodily solids. You don't even have to remove any bones first. And sir? Don't fret if what you see coming out of you don't look exactly like what you expect. If, for example, your pee turn into hundreds of little frogs and hop away to hide in the dark corners. Is how you folks say it? "Change is good." Right? Yahman.

Next stop is the Twinkling City. See all the rainbow colours as the light catch the oil slick? Pretty, nah true? Pickney-child, you too smart for me. You right. No light not in the sky to make refractions in the oil slick.

The actual city, of course, is down below the surface. Oonuh want to see? All right, I will open up one window. You gwine haffe peer out one at a time. Don't worry; I will stand by and make sure the murk don't reach long fingers in and pull you out for the mongooses. Oh! Out he gone! Why he open the window before I was ready? Never mind. I ready now. Who else want to look? Yes, lady. Lean out. I will grab your waist. If you screw up your y'eye-them and gaze hard, you might see thousands and thousands of lights flickering down below. We nah know where the electricity coming from to power the city, but there underneath the oil, it still going. Traffic lights still clicking from red to green and back again. Factories still a-run. I bet you anything the university still full up of scholars, experimenting on the wonders they find in the uprisen sea, and studying the results, and making discoveries, and arguing, and publishing.

Now, as I was saying to the rest of oonuh; the oil slick have a circumference of approximately three hundred and twenty-five square miles, and is about twenty-nine feet deep. I say, "oil slick" because is that it was at the beginning of the duppy tide, but like everything here, it change up. It have a way nowadays to rise up all of a sudden and grab sea gulls from out the air. At night, it will sometimes whisper to us in our dreams. Those who can't hear it have a way to die screaming before they wake up. Perhaps you already beginning to hear it when you sleeping? Show of hands? All of oonuh hearing it except that man in the noisy shirt? Maybe the shirt drowning out the sound of things you need to hear. Sir, when we get back to the resort, they will have a ticket waiting for you, for a flight home. You will have to leave right away, before night come. Your choice, though. Only try don't doze off between now and when we get back.

Come back in now, lady. My arms don't get tired, exactly, but put a tender life in my hands like this, and after a while, I start to get certain impulses. To let go, or to hold too tight. Quick, close the window!

Yes, of course I was here when the duppy tide make landfall. Is the reason I still here. On our TV stations, we had meteorologists telling us for days to get out, get out. Local weather website had a live feed. I would watch it on my phone during breaks at work, and on my computer when I was home in the evenings.

What? You think say "tropics" mean "backward"? Chuh.

The feed didn't look so bad, though. Long shots of dark sea and a dark sky. Screech of the wind whistling past the fixed camera. Camera view little bit unsteady from the wind making it vibrate. Nothing we never see before. Until I look at it good and realize the camera image not split into the usual two equal horizontal bars of slate sky on top of midnight sea. Up at the top of the image, a shallow bar of lighter grey. That was all the camera could see of the sky. The lower bar, the one taking up more than seven-eighths of the computer screen? That was the duppy tide rising up. I wait too long to leave. Most people did evacuate long since, but I couldn't find Malky. You sure you don't see him out there in the dark? Sometimes I think I spot him, but I can't really tell in the murk.

I couldn't leave him all alone.

We have to speed up. Time getting short. Over here in this boiling bay, all the fights we ever fight, for freedom, for independence, revolts against hunger, protests for wages.

That laughing waterfall? This land had stewards before us.

Rush, driver, rush past all of them. All the zombis. How many of oonuh know is this part of the world zombis come from? No hands. Well, you know now.

Finally. Last stop. I will let you out the bus just now, but don't get too close to the whirlpool. You haffe koo 'pon it from a distance. This island have a bedrock of ancient limestone, so we get sinkholes. Some terrible things get push down into sinkholes over the centuries; lost, and then forgotten. But that thing outside? That is all the sinkholes, with all their cargo. That is sinkhole papa. And yet, all the ocean it swallow, the levels only rising, not going down. Massa Fish the—well. I was going to say, "The Unflappable," but a fish had best be able to flap, you don't find? So. Massa Fish the Intensely Flappable. You feel him now? That vibration rumbling up through you, that sound too low to hear, but so deep it make your insides shiver? My generous guests, what you looking at is the open maw of Massa Fish. He shouting. He been shouting since the duppy tide beach him up here on the mountain. And me think say him finally getting an answer. Check the skyline. Dark. Seven-eighth's black, with a little grey line of sky on top. Duppy tide a-come down again, even vaster! Massa Fish a-call out for him mama! I so excited to see what changes she will bring this time, I could turn myself inside out! Any last questions, fish food?

How to escape the tide? Me sorry, friends; me don't have the answer.

I never did escape.

Jamaica Ginger

with Nisi Shawl

Editor Bill Campbell of Rosarium Press invited me to submit a piece to be considered for inclusion in Stories for Chip, *a fiction anthology in celebration of the writing of Samuel R. Delany (aka Chip).*

Chip is probably the person whose writing has had the most profound influence on me. I was being deeply moved by his work before I even discovered he was a black speculative fiction author—the first one of whom I was aware—and before I was out to myself as queer (he's gay, and representations of gay and queer existence feature a lot in his work). Chip is also a supreme literary stylist. His lyricism, his imagery, philosophical thought, and frankness of content have been bringing me joy and expanding my mind for decades. I had the great fortune of learning from him when I was a student at the Clarion Science Fiction and Fantasy Workshop. I believe that was in 1996. We have since become friends. Of course I wanted to write a story for Chip!

But I was exhausted, and at the end of my rope creatively. I knew I didn't have the stamina right then to write a short story. So I asked the brilliant Nisi Shawl whether they would like to cowrite one with me. They accepted, much to my delight. (After I'd discovered that Chip was black, I went searching for the other Black spec fic authors. There were only a handful at the time. One of the people I found was Nisi, whose first story "The Rainses'" had recently been published in Asimov's. *Nisi has been one of my touchstones ever since.) I had a notion to build something around Jamaica Ginger. It was a tonic sold during prohibition that the manufacturers deliberately adulterated with triorthocresyl phosphate, causing many to develop the degenerative nerve disease that came to be called "jake leg." Nisi suggested we reference Chip's novel* They Fly at Çiron *in our story. In addition, we both liked the idea of going teslapunk with the piece by mainstreaming some of the visionary technological advances the doomed inventor Nikolai Tesla was never able to take to market. And we agreed on bringing the lives of the post-Emancipation Black sleeping-car porters into the story. Nisi and I traded words and scenes back and forth. It was extraordinary to collaborate with them. "Jamaica Ginger" is the result.*

"Damn and blast it!"

Plaquette let herself in through the showroom door of the watchmaker's that morning to hear Msieur blistering the air of his shop with his swearing. The hulking clockwork man he'd been working on was high-stepping around the workroom floor in a clumsy lurch. It lifted its knees comically high, its body listing to one side and its feet coming down in the wrong order; toe, then heel. Billy Sumach, who delivered supplies to Msieur, was in the workroom. Through the open doorway he threw her a merry glance with his pretty brown eyes, but he had better sense than to laugh at Msieur's handiwork with Msieur in the room.

Msieur glared at Plaquette. "You're late. That's coming off your pay."

Plaquette winced. Their family needed every cent of her earnings, but she'd had to wait home till Ma got back from the railroad to take over minding Pa.

The mechanical George staggered tap-click, tap-click across the shop. It crashed into a wall and tumbled with a clank to the floor, then lay there whirring. Msieur swore again, words Ma would be mortified to know that Plaquette had heard. He snatched off one of his own shoes and threw it at the George. Billy Sumach gave a little peep of swallowed laughter. Msieur pointed at the George. "Fix it," he growled at Plaquette. "I have to present it to the governor the day after tomorrow."

As though Plaquette didn't know that. "Yes, Msieur," she said to his back as he stormed through the door to the showroom.

The second the door slammed shut, Billy let out a whoop. Plaquette found herself smiling along with him, glad of a little amusement. It was scarce in her life nowadays. "My land," Billy said, "'Pears Old George there has got himself the jake leg!"

The fun blew out of the room like a candle flame. "Don't you joke," Plaquette told him, through teeth clamped tight together. "You know 'bout my Pa."

Billy's face fell. "Oh Lord, Plaquette, I'm sorry."

"Just help me get this George to its feet. It weighs a ton."
Billy was a fine man, of Plaquette's colour and station. Lately
when he came by with deliveries, he'd been favouring her with
smiles and wistful looks. But she couldn't study that right now,
not with Pa taken so poorly. Together they wrestled the George
over to Plaquette's work table. There it stood. Its painted-on
porter's uniform had chipped at one shoulder when it fell. Its
chest door hung open as a coffin lid. Plaquette wanted to weep
at the tangle of metal inside it. She'd taken the George's chest
apart and put it back together, felt like a million times now.
Msieur couldn't see what was wrong, and neither could she.
Its arms worked just fine; Plaquette had strung the wires inside
them herself. But the legs. . . .

"You'll do it," Billy said. "Got a good head on your shoulders."

Feeling woeful, Plaquette nodded.

An uncomfortable silence held between them an instant. If
he wanted to come courting, now would be the time to ask.
Instead, he held up his clipboard. "Msieur gotta sign for these
boxes."

Plaquette nodded again. She wouldn't have felt right saying
yes to courting, anyway. Not with Pa so sick.

If he'd asked, that is.

"Billy, you ever think of doing something else?" The words
were out before she knew she wanted to ask them.

He frowned thoughtfully. "You know, I got cousins own a
lavender farm, out Des Allemands way. Sometimes I think I
might join them."

"Not some big city far off?" She wondered how Billy's cal-
loused hands would feel against her cheek.

"Nah. Too noisy, too dirty. Too much like this place." Then
he saw her face. "Though if a pretty girl like you were there," he

said slowly, as though afraid to speak his mind, "I guess I could come to love it."

He looked away then. "Think Msieur would mind me popping to the showroom real quick? I could take him his shoe."

"Just make sure no white folks in there."

Billy collected Msieur's shoe, then ducked into the showroom. Plaquette hung her hat on the hook near the back and sat down to work. Msieur's design for the George lay crumpled on her table where he'd left it. She smoothed out the sheets of paper and set to poring over them, as she'd done every day since she started working on the George. This was the most intricate device Msieur had ever attempted. It had to perform flawlessly on the day the governor unveiled it at the railroad. For a couple years now, Msieur had depended on Plaquette's keen vision and small, deft hands to assemble the components of his more intricate timepieces and his designs. By the point he decided to teach her how to read his notes, she'd already figured out how to decipher most of the symbols and his chicken-scratch writing.

There. That contact strip would never sit right, not lying flat like that. Needed a slight bend to it. Plaquette got a pencil out of her table's drawer and made a correction to Msieur's notes. Billy came back and started to bring boxes from his cart outside in through the workroom door. While he worked and tried to make small talk with her, Plaquette got herself a tray. From the drawers of the massive oak watchmaker's cabinet in the middle of the shop, she collected the items she needed and took them to her bench.

"Might rain Saturday, don't you think?" huffed Billy as he heaved a box to the very top of the pile.

"Might," Plaquette replied. "Might not." His new bashfulness

with her made her bashful in return. They couldn't quite seem
to be companionable any more. She did a last check of the
long row of black velvet cloth on her workbench, hundreds of
tiny brass and crystal components gleaming against the black
fur of the fabric. She knew down to the last how many cogs,
cams, and screws were there. She had to. Msieur counted every
penny, fussed over every quarter inch of the fine gauge wire
that went into the timekeepers his shop produced. At year's end
he tallied every watch finding, every scrap of leather. If any
were missing, the cost was docked from her salary. Kind of the
backwards of a Christmas bonus. As if Msieur didn't each evening collect sufficient profits from his till and lower them into
his "secret" safe.

Billy saw Plaquette pick up her tweezers and turn toward
the mechanical porter. "Do you want Claude?" he asked her.

He knew her so well. She smiled at him. "Yes, please." He
leapt to go fetch Claude out of the broom closet where they
stored him.

Billy really was sweet, and he wasn't the only one who'd
begun looking at her differently as she filled out from girl to
woman this past year. Ma said she had two choices: Marry Billy
and be poor but in love, or angle to become Msieur's placée
and take up life in the Quarter. Msieur would never publicly
acknowledge her or any children he had by her, but she would
be comfortable, and maybe pass some of her comforts along
to Ma and Pa.

Not that they would ever ask. 'Sides, she wasn't even sure
she was ready to be thinking about all that bother just yet.

Plaquette yawned. She was bone-tired, and no wonder. She'd
been spending her nights and Sundays looking after Pa since
he had come down with the jake leg.

Claude's books had excited Plaquette when she first heard them, but in time they'd become overly familiar. She knew every thrilling leap from crumbling clifftops, every graveside confession, every switched and secret identity that formed part of those well-worn tales. They had started to grate on her, those stories of people out in the world, having adventures she never could. Pa got to see foreign places; the likes of New York and Chicago and San Francisco. He only passed through them, of course. He had to remain on the train. But he got to see new passengers at each stop, to smell foreign air, to look up into a different sky. Or he had.

He would again, when he got better. He would. The metal Georges would need minding, wouldn't they? And who better for that job than Pa, who'd been a dependable George himself these many years?

But for Plaquette, there was only day after day, one marching in sequence behind another, in this workroom. Stringing tiny, shiny pieces of metal together. Making shift nowadays to always be on the other side of the room from Msieur whenever he was present. She was no longer the board-flat young girl she'd been when she first went to work for Msieur. She'd begun to bud, and Msieur seemed inclined to pluck himself a tender placée flower to grace his lapel. A left-handed marriage was one thing, but to a skinflint like Msieur?

Problems crowding up on each other like storm clouds running ahead of the wind. Massing so thick that Plaquette couldn't presently see her way through them. Ma said when life got dark like that, all's you could do was keep putting one foot in front the other and hope you walked yourself to somewhere brighter.

But as usual, once Billy set Claude up and the automaton

began its recitation, her work was accurate and quick. She loved the challenge and ritual of assemblage: laying exactly the right findings out on the cloth; listening to the clicking sound of Claude's gears as he recited one of his scrolls; letting the ordered measure take her thoughts away till all that was left was the precise dance of her fingers as they selected the watch parts and clicked, screwed, or pinned them into place. Sometimes she only woke from her trance of time, rhythm, and words when Msieur shook her by the shoulder come evening and she looked up to realize the whole day had gone by.

Shadows fell on Plaquette's hands, obscuring her work. She looked around, blinking. When had it gone dusk? The workroom was empty. Billy had probably gone on about his other business hours ago. Claude's scroll had run out and he'd long since fallen silent. Why hadn't Msieur told her it was time to go? She could hear him wandering around his upstairs apartment.

She rubbed her burning eyes. He'd probably hoped she'd keep working until the mechanical George was set to rights.

Had she done it? She slid her hands out of the wire-and-cam guts of the mechanical man. She'd have to test him to be sure. But in the growing dark, she could scarcely make out the contacts in the George's body that needed to be tripped in order to set it in motion.

Plaquette rose from her bench, stretched her twinging back and frowned—in imitation of Mama—through the doorway at the elaborately decorated Carcel lamp displayed in the shop's front. Somewhat outmoded though it was, the clockwork regulating the lamp's fuel supply and draft served Msieur as one of many proofs of his meticulous handiwork—her meticulous handiwork. If she stayed in the workshop any later, she'd have to light that lamp. And for all that he wanted her to work late,

Msieur would be sure to deduct the cost of the oil used from her wages. He could easily put a vacuum bulb into the Carcel, light it with cheap units of tesla power instead of oil, but he mistrusted energy he couldn't see. Said it wasn't "refined."

She took a few steps in the direction of the Carcel.

C-RRR-EEEAK!

Plaquette gasped and dashed for the showroom door to the street. She had grabbed the latch rope before her wits returned. She let the rope go and faced back toward the black doorway out of which emerged the automaton, Claude. It rocked forward on its treads, left side, right. Its black velvet jacket swallowed what little light there still was. But the old-fashioned white ruff circling its neck cast up enough brightness to show its immobile features. They had, like hers, much of the African to them. Claude came to a stop in front of her.

CRREAK!

Plaquette giggled. "You giving me a good reminder—I better put that oil on your wheels as well as your insides. You like to scare me half to death rolling round the dark in here." She pulled the miniature oil tin from her apron pocket and knelt to lubricate the wheels of the rolling treads under Claude's platform. It had been Plaquette's idea to install them to replace the big brass wheels he'd had on either side. She'd grown weary of righting Claude every time he rolled over an uneven surface and toppled. It had been good practice, though, for nowadays, when Pa was like to fall with each spastic step he took, and Plaquette so often had to catch him. He hated using the crutches. And all of this because he'd begun taking a few sips of jake to warm his cold bones before his early morning shifts.

Jamaica Ginger was doing her family in, that was sure.

Her jostling of Claude must have released some last dregs of energy left in his winding mechanism, for just then he took it into his mechanical head to drone, ". . . nooot to escaaape it by exerrrtion . . ."

Quickly, Plaquette stopped the automaton midsentence. For good measure, she removed the book from its spool inside Claude. She didn't want Msieur to hear that she was still downstairs, alone in the dark.

As Plaquette straightened again, a new thought struck her.

The shutters folded back easily. White light from the coil-powered street lamp outside flooded the tick-tocking showroom, glittering on glass cases and gold and brass watches, on polished wooden housings and numbered faces like pearly moons. More than enough illumination for Plaquette's bright eyes. "Come along, Claude," Plaquette commanded as she headed back toward the workroom—somewhat unnecessarily, as she had Claude's wardenclyffe in the pocket of her leather work apron. Where it went, Claude was bound to follow. Which made it doubly foolish of her to have been startled by him.

She could see the mechanical porter more clearly now, its cold steel body painted deep blue in imitation of a porter's uniform, down to the gold stripes at the cuffs of the jacket. Its perpetually smiling black face. The Pullman porter "cap" atop its head screwed on like a bottle top. Inside it was the tesla receiver the George would use to guide itself around inside the sleeping-car cabins the Pullman company planned to outfit with wireless transmitters. That part had been Plaquette's idea. Msieur had grumbled, but Plaquette could see him mentally adding up the profits this venture could bring him.

If Msieur's George was a success, that'd be the end of her father's job. Human porters had human needs. A mechanical

George would rarely be ill, never miss work. Would always smile, would never need a new uniform—just the occasional paint touch-up. Would need to be paid for initially, but never paid thereafter.

With two fingers, Plaquette poked the George's ungiving chest. The mechanical man didn't so much as rock on its sturdy legs. Plaquette still thought treads would have been better, like Claude's. But Msieur wanted the new Georges to be as lifelike as possible, so as not to scare the fine white ladies and gentlemen who rode the luxury sleeping cars. So the Georges must be able to walk. Smoothly, like Pa used to.

The chiming clocks in the showroom began tolling the hour, each in their separate tones. Plaquette gasped. Though surrounded by clocks, she had completely forgotten how late it was. Ma would be waiting for her; it was nearly time for Pa's shift at the station! She couldn't stop now to test the George. She slapped Claude's wardenclyffe into his perpetually outstretched hand, pulled her bonnet onto her head, and hastened outside, stopping only to jiggle the shop's door by its polished handle to make sure the latch had safely caught.

Only a few blocks to scurry home under the steadily burning lamps, among the sparse clumps of New Orleans's foreign sightseers and those locals preferring to conduct their business in the cool of night. In her hurry, she bumped into one overdressed gent. He took her by the arms and leered, looking her up and down. She muttered an apology and pulled away before he could do more than that. She was soon home, where Ma was waiting on the landing outside their rooms. The darkness and Pa's hat and heavy coat disguised Ma well enough to fool the white supervisors for a while, and the other colored were in on the secret. But if Ma came in late—

"Don't fret, Darling," Ma said, bending to kiss Plaquette's cheek. "I can still make it. He ate some soup and I just help him to the necessary, so he probably sleep till morning."

Plaquette went into the dark apartment. No fancy lights for them. Ma had left the kerosene lamp on the kitchen table, turned down low. Plaquette could see through to Ma and Pa's bed. Pa was tucked in tight, only his head showing above the covers. He was breathing heavy, not quite a snore. The shape of him underneath the coverlet looked so small. Had he shrunk, or was she growing?

Plaquette hung up her hat. In her hurry to get home, she'd left Msieur's still wearing her leather apron. As she pulled it off to hang it beside her hat, something inside one of the pockets thumped dully against the wall. One of Claude's book scrolls; the one she'd taken from him. She returned it to the pocket. Claude could have it back tomorrow. She poured herself some soup from the pot on the stove. Smelled like pea soup and crawfish, with a smoky hint of ham. Ma had been stretching the food with peas, seasoning it with paper-thin shavings from that one ham shank for what seemed like weeks now. Plaquette didn't think she could stomach the taste of more peas, more stingy wisps of ham. What she wouldn't give for a good slice of roast beef, hot from the oven, its fat glistening on the plate.

Her stomach growled, not caring. Crawfish soup would suit it just fine. Plaquette sat to table and set about spooning cold soup down her gullet. The low flame inside the kerosene lamp flickered, drawing pictures. Plaquette imagined she saw a tower, angels circling it (or demons), a war raging below. Men skewering other men with blades and spears. Beasts she'd never before heard tell of, lunging—

"Girl, what you seeing in that lamp? Have you so seduced."

Plaquette started and pulled her mind out of the profane world in the lamp. "Pa!" She jumped up from the table and went to kiss him on the forehead. He hugged her, his hands flopping limply to thump against her back. He smelled of sweat, just a few days too old to be ignored. "You need anything? The necessary?"

"Naw." He tried to pat the bed beside him, failed. He grimaced. "Just come and sit by me a little while. Tell me the pictures in your mind."

"If I do, you gotta tell me 'bout San Francisco again." She sat on the bed facing him, knees drawn up beneath her skirts like a little child.

"Huh. I'm never gonna see that city again." It tore at Plaquette's heart to see his eyes fill with tears. "Oh, Plaquette," he whispered, "what are we gonna do?"

Not we; her. She would do it. "Hush, Pa." It wouldn't be Billy. Ma and Pa were showing her that you couldn't count on love and hard work alone to pull you through. Not when this life would scarcely pay a coloured man a penny to labour all his days and die young. She patted Pa's arm, took his helpless hand in hers. She closed her eyes to recollect the bright story in the lamp flame. Opened them again. "So. Say there's a tower, higher than that mountain you told me 'bout that one time. The one with the clouds all round the bottom of it so it look to be floating?"

Pa's mouth was set in bitterness. He stared off at nothing. For a moment, Plaquette though he wouldn't answer her. But then, his expression unchanged, he ground out, "Mount Rainier. In Seattle."

"That's it. This here tower, it's taller than that."

Pa turned his eyes to hers. "What's it for?"

"How should I know? I'll tell you that when it comes to me. I know this, though; there's people flying round that tower, right up there in the air. Like men, and maybe a woman, but with wings. Like angels. No, like bats."

Pa's eyes grew round. The lines in his face smoothed out as Plaquette spun her story. A cruel prince. A fearsome army. A lieutenant with a conscience.

It would have to be Msieur.

That ended up being a good night. Pa fell back to sleep, his face more peaceful than she'd seen in days. Plaquette curled up against his side. She was used to his snoring and the heaviness of his drugged breath. She meant to sleep there beside him, but her mind wouldn't let her rest. It was full of imaginings: dancing with Msieur at the Orleans Ballroom, her wearing a fine gown and a fixed, automaton smile; Billy's hopeful glances and small kindnesses, his endearingly nervous bad jokes; and Billy's shoulders, already bowed at seventeen from lifting and hauling too-heavy boxes day in, day out, tick, tock, forever (how long before her eyesight went from squinting at tiny watch parts?); an army of tireless metal Georges, more each day, replacing the fleshly porters, and brought about in part by her cleverness. Whichever path her future took, Plaquette could only see disaster.

Yet in the air above her visions, they flew.

Finally Plaquette eased herself out of bed. The apartment was dark; she'd long since blown out the lamp to save wick and oil. She tiptoed carefully to the kitchen. By feel, she got Claude's reading scroll out of the pocket of her apron. She crept out onto the landing. By the light of a streetlamp, she unrolled and rerolled it so that she could see the end of the book. The

punched holes stopped a good foot-and-a-half before the end
of the roll. There was that much blank space left.

Plaquette knew *My Lady Nobody* practically word for word.
She studied the roll, figuring out the patterns of holes that created the sounds that allowed Claude to speak the syllables of
the story. She could do this. She crept back inside and felt her
way through the kitchen drawer. She grasped something way
at the back. A bottle, closed tight, some liquid still sloshing
around inside it. A sniff of the lid told her what it was. She put
the bottle aside and kept rummaging through the drawer. Her
heart beat triple-time when she found what she was looking
for. Pa did indeed have more than one ticket punch.

It was as though there was a fever rising in her; for the next
few hours she crouched shivering on the landing and in a frenzy, punched a complicated pattern into the end of the scroll,
stopping every so often to roll it back to the beginning for
guidance on how to punch a particular syllable. By the time
she'd used up the rest of the roll, her fingers were numb with
cold, her teeth chattering, the sky was going pink in the east,
and the landing was scattered with little circles of white card.
But her brain finally felt at peace.

She rose stiffly to her feet. A light breeze began blowing the
white circles away. Ma would probably be home in another
hour or so. Plaquette replaced the scroll in her apron pocket,
changed into her nightgown, and lay back down beside her
father. In seconds, she fell into a deep, dreamless sleep.

Ma woke her all too soon. Plaquette's eyes felt like there was
grit in them. Pa was still snoring away. Ma gestured her out

to the kitchen, where they could speak without waking him. Ma's face was drawn with fatigue. She'd spent the night fetching and carrying for white people. "How he doing?" she asked.

"Tolerable. Needs a bath."

Ma sighed. "I know. He won't let me wash him. He ashamed."

Plaquette felt her eyebrows lift in surprise. The Pa she knew washed every morning and night and had a full bath on Sundays.

Ma pulled a chair out from under the table and thumped herself down into it. Her lips were pinched together with worry. "He not getting better."

"We're managing."

"I thought he might mend. Some do. Tomorrow he supposed to start his San Francisco run. Guess I gotta do it."

At first, Plaquette felt only envy. Even Ma was seeing the world. Then she understood the problem. "San Francisco run's five days."

Ma nodded. "I know you can see to him all by yourself, darling. You're a big girl. But you gotta go to work for Msieur, too. Your Pa, he's not ready to be alone all day."

It was one weight too many on the scales. Plaquette feared it would tip her completely over. She stammered, "I-I have to-to go, Ma." Blindly, she grabbed her bonnet and apron and sped out the door. Guilt followed her the whole way to Msieur's. Leaving Ma like that.

She would have to start charming Msieur, sooner rather than later.

Plaquette was the first one to the shop, just as she'd planned it. Msieur generally lingered over his breakfast, came down in time to open the showroom to custom. She'd have a few minutes to herself. She'd make it up to Ma later. Sit down with her and Pa Sunday morning and work out a plan.

Claude and the George were beside her bench, right where she'd left them. She bent and patted Claude on the cheek. She delved into Claude's base through its open hatch and removed the remaining three "books" that Claude recited when the rolls of punched paper were fed into his von Kempelen apparatus. Claude bided open and silent, waiting to be filled with words. Eagerly Plaquette lowered her book onto the spool and locked that in place, then threaded the end—no, the beginning, the very beginning of this new story—onto the toothed drum of the von Kempelen and closed its cover.

She removed the ribbon bearing Claude's key from his wrist. She wound him tight and released the guard halfway— for some of the automaton's mechanisms were purely for show. In this mode, Claude's carven lips would remain unmoving.

With a soft creak, the spool began to turn. A flat voice issued from beneath Claude's feet:

"*They Fly at Çironia*, by Della R. Mausney. Prologue. Among the tribes and villages—"

It was working!

Afire with the joy of it, Plaquette began working on the George again.

But come noon the metal man was still as jake-legged as Pa. Seemed there was nothing Plaquette could do to fix either one.

She tried to settle her thoughts. She couldn't work if her mind was troubled. She'd listened to her punch-card story three times today already. She knew she was being vain, but she purely loved hearing her words issue forth from Claude. The story was a creation that was completely hers, not built on the carcass of someone else's ingenuity. Last night's sleepless frenzy had cut the bonds on her imagination. She'd set free something she didn't know she had in her. Claude's other novels were all rich folk weeping over rich folk problems, white folk pitching woo. *They Fly at Çironia* was different, wickedly so. The sweep and swoop of it. The crudeness, the brutality.

She wound the key set into Claude's side until it was just tight enough, and tripped the release fully. With a quiet sound like paper riffling, Claude's head started to move. His eyelids flicked up and down. His head turned left to right. The punch card clicked forward one turn. Claude's jaw opened, and he began to recite.

"Now," she whispered to the George, "one more time. Let's see what's to be done with you." She reached into his chest with her tweezers as the familiar enchantment began to come upon her. While the Winged Ones *screeed* through the air of Çironia's mountains on pinions of quartz, Plaquette wove and balanced quiltings of coiled springs, hooked them into layer upon layer of delicately weighted controls, dropped them into one another's curving grasps, adjusted and readjusted the workings of the George's legs.

Finally, for the fourth time that day, the Winged Ones seized the story's teller and tossed him among themselves in play. Finally, for the fourth time that day, he picked himself up from the ground, gathered about himself such selfness as he could.

The short book ended. Gradually Plaquette's trance did the same.

Except for the automatons, she was alone. The time was earlier than it had been last night. Not by much. Shadows filled the wide corners, and the little light that fell between buildings to slip in at the tall windows was thin and nearly useless.

A creaking board revealed Msieur's presence in the showroom just before the door communicating with it opened. He stuck his head through, smiling like the overdressed man Plaquette had run from on her way home last night. She returned the smile, trying for winsomeness.

"Not taking ill, are you?" Msieur asked. So much for her winning ways.

He moved forward into the room to examine the George. "Have you finished for the day? I doubt you made much progress." His manicured hands reopened the chest she had just shut. He bent as if to peer inside, but his eyes slid sideways, toward Plaquette's bosom and shoulders. She should stand proud to show off her figure. Instead, she stumbled up from her bench and edged behind the stolid protection of Claude's metal body.

Smiling more broadly yet, Msieur turned his gaze to the George's innards in reality. "You do appear to have done something, however—let's test it!" He closed up the chest access. He retrieved the mechanism's key from the table, wound it tight, and tripped its initial release. The George lumbered clumsily to its feet.

"Where's that instruction card? Ah!" Msieur inserted it and pressed the secondary release button.

A grinding hum issued from the metal chest. The George's left knee lifted—waist-high—higher! But then it lowered and the foot kicked out. It landed heel first. One step—another— a third—a fourth—four more—it stopped. It had reached the workroom's far wall, and, piled against it, the Gladstones and imperials it was now supposed to load itself with. It whirred and stooped. It ticked and reached, tocked and grasped, and then—

Then it stuck in place. Quivering punctuated by rhythmic jerks ran along its blue-painted frame. Rrrr-rap! Rrrr-rap!

RRRR-RAP! With each repetition the noise of the George's faulty operation grew louder. Msieur ran quickly to disengage its power.

"Such precision! Astonishing!" Msieur appeared pleased at even partial success. He stroked his neat, silky beard thought-fully. He seemed to come to a decision. "We'll work through the night. The expense of the extra oil consumed is nothing if we succeed—and I believe we will."

By "we," Msieur meant her. He expected for her to toil on his commission all night.

But what about Pa?

Self-assured though he was, Msieur must have sensed her hesitation. "What do you need? Of course—you must be fed! I'll send to the Café du Monde—" He glanced around the empty workshop. "—or if I must go myself, no matter. A cup of chicory and a slice of chocolate pie, girl! How does that sound?"

Chocolate pie! But as she opened her mouth to assent she found herself saying instead, "But Ma—Pa—"

Msieur was already in the showroom; she heard the muffled bell that rang whenever he slid free the drawer holding the day's receipts. Plaquette crept forward; obediently, Claude fol-lowed her onto the crimson carpet. Startled, Msieur thrust his hands below the counter so she couldn't see what they held. "What's that you say?"

"My folks will worry if I don't get home 'fore too late. I better—"

"No. You stay. I'll have the Café send a messenger."

That wouldn't help. She couldn't say why, though, so she had to let Msieur herd her back to the workroom. Under his suspi-cious eye she wound up the George again and walked it to her bench. Not long after, Claude rejoined her. "That's right," said Msieur, satisfied. "And if this goes well, I'll have a proposition to make to your mother. Eh? You have been quite an asset to me. I should like to, erm, deepen our connection."

Plaquette swallowed. "Yes, Msieur."

His face brightened. "Yes? Your own place in the Quarter. You would keep working in the shop, of course. Splendid, then. Splendid." He winked at her! The door to the showroom slammed shut. The jangle of keys told Plaquette that Msieur had locked her in. Like a faint echo, the door to the street slammed seconds later.

She sank back onto her seat. Only greyness, like dirty water, trickled in at the workroom windows, fading as she watched.

So even if she became Msieur's placée, tended to their left-hand marriage, he would expect her to continue in this dreary workroom.

Plaquette frowned, attempting to recall if she'd heard the grate and clank of the safe's door closing on the day's proceeds, the money and precious jewels Msieur usually hid away there. Sometimes she could remember what had happened around her during the last few minutes of her trance.

Not today.

Only the vague outlines of its windows broke the darkening workroom's walls. And beneath where she knew the showroom door stood, a faint, blurry smear gleamed dully, vanishing remnant of l'heure bleue. She must go home now. Before Msieur returned with his chocolate pie and his unctuous wooing.

She considered the showroom door a moment longer. But the door from there led right to the street. People would be bound to see her escape. The workroom door, then; the delivery entrance that led to the alleyway. She twisted to face it.

Msieur had reinforced this door the same summer when, frightened of robbers, he sank his iron safe beneath the workroom's huge oak cabinet. It was faced outside with bricks, a feeble attempt at concealment that made it heavy—too heavy for Plaquette alone to budge. Plaquette, however, was not alone.

Marshaling the George into position, she set him to kick down the thick workroom door. The George walked forward a few more feet, then stopped there in the alley, lacking for further commands. A dumb mechanical porter with no more sense than a headless chicken.

Though she hadn't planned it, Plaquette found she knew what she wanted to do next. She rushed back to her bench. Claude cheerfully rocked after her. She erased all the corrections that she'd meticulously made to Msieur's notes. She scribbled in new ones, any nonsense that came to mind. Without her calculations Msieur would never work out the science of making a wireless iron George. Someone else eventually might, but this way, it wouldn't be on Plaquette's conscience.

She took a chair with her out into the alleyway, climbed up onto it, and unscrewed the George's cap. She upturned it so that it sat like a bowl on the George's empty head. From her apron she produced the bottle she'd taken from Ma's kitchen; the one with the dregs of jake in it. Ma could never bear to throw anything away, even poison. Plaquette poured the remaining jake all over the receiver inside the George's cap. There was a satisfying sizzling sound of wires burning out. Jake leg this, you son of a—well. Ma wouldn't like her even thinking such language. She screwed the cap back onto the George's head. Msieur might never discover the sabotage.

One more trip back inside the workroom, to Claude's broom closet. On a hook in there hung the Pullman porter's uniform that Msieur had been given to model the George's painted costume after. It was a men's small. A little large on her, but she belted in the waist and rolled up the trouser hems. She slid her hands into the trouser pockets, and exclaimed in delight. So much room! Not dainty, feminine pockets—bigger even than those stitched onto her workroom apron. She could carry almost anything she pleased in these!

But now she really must hurry. She strewed her clothing about the workroom—let Msieur make of that what he would. A kidnapping or worse, her virgin innocence soiled, maybe her lifeless body dumped in the bayou. And off they went—Plaquette striding freely in her masculine get-up, one foot in front of the other, making her plan as she made up the stories she told Pa: by letting the elements come to her in the moment. Claude rolled in her wake, tipping dangerously forward as he negotiated the steep drop from banquette to roadway, falling farther and farther behind.

When they came to the stairs up the side of the building where she lived, she was stumped for what to do. Claude was not the climbing sort. For the moment she decided to store him in the necessary—she'd figure out how to get him back to Msieur's later. She'd miss his cheerful face, though.

Ma yelped when a stranger in a porter's uniform walked in the door. She reached for her rolling pin.

"Ma! It just me!" Plaquette pulled off her cap, let her hair bush out free from under it.

Ma boggled. "Plaquette? Why you all got up like that?"

The sound of Pa's laughter rasped from her parents' bedroom. Pa was sitting up in bed, peering through the doorway. "That's my hellcat girl," he said. "Mother, you ain't got to go out on the Frisco run. Plaquette gon' do it."

Ma stamped her foot at him. "Don't be a fool! She doing no such thing."

Except she was! Till now, Plaquette hadn't thought it through. But that's exactly what she was going to do.

Ma could read the determination in her face. "Child, don't you see? It won't work. You too young to pass for your Pa. Gonna get him fired."

Plaquette thought fast. "Not Pa. Pa's replacement." She pulled herself up to her full height. "Pleased to introduce you to Mule Aranslyde, namely myself. Ol' Pullman's newest employee." She sketched a mock bow. Pa cackled in delight.

A little plate of peas and greens and ham fat had been set aside for her. Plaquette spooned it down while Ma went on about how Plaquette must have lost her everlovin' mind and Pa wasn't helping with his nonsense. Then Plaquette took a still-protesting Ma by the hand and led her into the bedroom. "Time's running short," she said. "Lemme tell y'all why I need to go." That brought a bit more commotion, though she didn't even tell them the half of it. Just the bit about the George. And she maybe said she'd broken it by accident.

Ma twisted Plaquette's long braids into a tight little bun and crammed them under the cap. "Don't know how you gonna fake doin Pa's job," she fretted. "Ain't as easy as it looks. I messed up so many times, supervisor asked me if I been in the whiskey. Nearly got your Pa fired."

Plaquette took Ma's two hands in her own. "I'm a 'prentice, remember?" She patted the letter in her breast pocket that Pa had dictated to her, the one telling Pa's porter friend Jonas

Jones who she was and to look out for her and thank you God bless you. She kissed Pa goodbye. Ma walked her out onto the landing, and that's when Plaquette's plan began to go sideways. There at the foot of the stairs was Claude, backing up and ramming himself repeatedly into the bottom stair. Plaquette had forgotten she had Claude's wardenclyffe in her pocket. All this time he'd been trying to follow it.

"Plaquette," said Ma, "what for you steal Msieur's machine?" It wasn't a shout but a low, scared, angry murmur—far worse. In the lamplight scattered into the yard from the main street, Claude's white-gloved hands glowed eerily.

Plaquette clattered down the stairs to confront the problem.

"I know you think he yours, but girl, he don't belong to you!" Ma had come down behind her. Plaquette didn't even need to turn to know the way Ma was looking at her: hard as brass and twice as sharp.

"I—I set him to follow me." Plaquette faltered for words. This was the part she hadn't told them.

Ma only said, "Oh, Lord. We in for it now."

Pa replied, "Maybe not."

"Watch where you're going!"

Plaquette muttered an apology to the man she'd jostled. Even late like this—it must have been nearly midnight—New Orleans's Union Station was thronged with travelers. But in Ma's wake Plaquette and Claude made slow yet steady headway through the chattering crowds. A makeshift packing crate disguised her mechanical friend; Plaquette held a length of clothesline that was supposed to fool onlookers into thinking she hauled it along. Of course the line kept falling slack. Ma looked back over her shoulder for the thirteenth time since they'd left home. But it couldn't be much farther now to the storage room where Pa had said they could hide Claude overnight. Or for a little longer. But soon as the inevitable hue and cry over his disappearance died down, Plaquette could return him to Msieur's. So long as no one discovered Claude where they were going to stash him—

"Stop! Stop! Thief!" Angry as she'd feared, Msieur's shout came from behind them. It froze her one long awful second before she could run.

Ahead Ma shoved past a fat man in woollens and sent him staggering to the right. Behind them came more exclamations, more men calling for them to halt, their cries mixed with the shrieks and swearing of the people they knocked aside. How'd he know where to look for her? Trust a man whose business was numbers to put two and two together. Msieur had friends with him—how many? Plaquette barely glanced back. Two? Four? No telling—she had to run to stay in front of Claude so he'd follow her to—an opening! She broke away from the thick-packed travelers and ran after Ma to a long brick walk between two puffing engines. Good. Cover. This must be why Ma had taken such an unexpected path. Swaying like a drunk in a hurricane, Claude in his crate lumbered after her.

The noise of their pursuers fell to a murmur. Maybe she'd lost them?

But when Plaquette caught up with Ma, Ma smacked her fists together and screamed. "No! Why you follow me over here? Ain't I told you we putting your fool mistake in the storage the other side of the tracks?"

"B-but you came this w-w-ay!" Plaquette stammered.

"I was creating a distraction for you to escape!"

The clatter and thump of running feet sounded clear again above the engines' huff and hiss. Coming closer. Louder. Louder. Ma threw her hands in the air. "We done! Oh, baby, you too young for jail!"

One of the dark train carriages Plaquette had run past had been split up the middle—hadn't it? A deeper darkness—a partially open door? Spinning, she rushed back the way they'd come. Yes! "Ma!" Plaquette pushed the sliding door hard as she could. It barely budged. Was that wide enough? She jumped and grabbed its handle and swung herself inside.

But Claude! Prisoned in slats, weighed down by his treads, he bumped disconsolately against the baggage car's high bottom. Following her and the wardenclyffe, exactly as programmed. Should she drop it? She dug through the deep pockets frantically and pulled it out so fast it flew from her hand and landed clattering somewhere in the carriage's impenetrable darkness.

Hidden like she wished she could hide from the hoarsely shouting men. But they sounded frustrated as well as angry now, and no nearer. Maybe the engine on the track next to this was in their way?

The train began moving. From Plaquette's perch it looked like the bricks and walkway rolled off behind her. Claude kept futile pace. The train was pulling up alongside Ma, standing hopelessly where Plaquette had left her, waiting to be caught. Now she was even with them. Plaquette brushed her fingers over Ma's yellow headscarf. It fell out of reach. "Goodbye, Ma! Just walk away from Claude! They won't know it was you!" Fact was, Plaquette felt excited almost as much as she was scared. Even if Msieur got past whatever barrier kept them apart right now, she was having her adventure!

The train stopped. Plaquette's heart just about did, too. Her only adventure would be jail. How could she help Ma and Pa from inside the pokey? She scanned the walkway for Msieur and his friends, coming to demand justice.

But no one showed. The shouts for her and Ma to stop grew fainter. The train started again, more slowly. Suddenly Ma was there, yanking Claude desperately by his cord. She'd pulled his crate off. It was on the platform, slowly disappearing into the distance. Together, Ma and Plaquette lifted Claude like he was luggage, tilting him to scrape over the carriage's narrow threshold. As they did, the tray holding the books caught on the edge and was dragged open—and it held more than book scrolls. Cool metallic disks, crisp or greasy slips of paper— Msieur's money!

How? Plaquette wasted a precious moment wondering—he must have put the day's take into Claude when she surprised him in the showroom.

Ma's eyes got wide as saucers. She was still running to keep up, puffing as she hefted Claude's weight. With a heave, she and Plaquette hauled him into the car. He landed with a heavy thump. The train was speeding up. There was no time to count it; Plaquette fisted up two handsful of the money, coins and bills both, and shoved it into Ma's hands. Surely it was enough to suffice Ma and Pa for a while. "I'll come back," she said.

The train kept going, building speed. Ma stopped running. She was falling behind fast. "You a good girl!" she yelled.

When it seemed sure the train wasn't stopping again any-time soon, Plaquette stuck her head out—a risk. A yellow gleam in the shadows was all she could see of Ma. Plaquette shoved the sliding door closed.

Well. She'd gone and done it now. Pa's note was no use;

this wasn't the train making the Frisco run. It for sure wasn't no sleeping-car train. A porter had no business here. The train could be going to the next town, or into the middle of next week. She had no way of knowing right now. For some reason, that made her smile.

She fumbled her way to Claude's open drawer. The money left in there was all coins, more than she could hold in one hand. She divided it among the deep, deep pockets in her trousers and jacket.

She was a true and actual thief, and a saboteur.

Finally she found the wardenclyffe. Feeling farther around her in the loud blackness, she determined the carriage was loaded as she'd imagined with trunks, suitcases, parcels of all shapes and sizes. Nothing comfortable as the beds at home, the big one or the little. She didn't care.

When the train stopped, she'd count the money. When the train stopped, she'd calculate what to do, where to go, how to get by. She could slip off anywhere, buy herself new clothes, become a new person.

She settled herself as well as she could on a huge, well-stuffed suitcase and closed her eyes.

Claude would help. She would punch more books for him to read and collect from the people who came to listen. Send money home to Pa and Ma every few weeks.

She'd write the books herself. She'd get him to punch them. She'd punch a set of instructions for how to punch instructions for punching. She'd punch another set of instructions and let Claude write books, too. And maybe come back one day soon. Find Billy. Take him away and show him a new life.

Waving at Trains

This story evolved from my notion that people who wave at passing trains are actually giving the passengers pieces of themselves to transport to the train's future destination. In effect they're saying, "I'm stuck here in one place, but maybe you'll permit this tiny essence of me to travel with you?" Then the Boston Review *invited me to submit a story. The story that follows is what grew from that kernel.*

SUMMERS, PRIITHI AND I were on our own while our parents were at work. We would meet in the corner of the playground, by that big old tamarind tree; you know the one? When it was close to tamarind season, and the fruit green and hard on the tree, the boys from the boys' school across the way would pick the unripe tamarind pods and pelt the girls from our school with them, till the caretaker came and shooed them away. By the time summer holidays came around, any fruit left on the tree would ripen, getting fat and brown. Then they would just

fall to the ground, cracking their brittle shells open when they
landed. Ants and mongooses would feed on the broken fruit.

Today the tropical sun was beating down warm on my
head—Priithi would scold me for not wearing my hat—and
my sandals kicked up grey dirt with each step, powdering my
bare legs almost to the knee. I stopped to pull the belt tighter
around the waistband of the khaki shorts I was wearing. They
were my brother's, way too big for me. The pockets sagged and
the pants' hems came almost to my knees. But Priithi said khaki would be better for walking and climbing in than my light
sundresses, and along with the brown T-shirt I was wearing, I
would be harder to spot when we got into the bush. She said
all those bright flower patterns I liked to wear wouldn't be any
good. She was probably right. Too besides, those big pockets
would be good for carrying pelting stones in, and the pocket
knife I had found in the back of a kitchen drawer at home.

Something was smelling real bad in the underbrush by the
side of the road. At first, the back of my neck went cold. But
then I realized that the rotten smell was more cooked than
raw; like when you drop an egg into a frying pan with hot oil
in it before you realize that the egg spoil. Whatever was hidden by the crackly, dried-up scrub over there, it wasn't moving
any more.

Still. No cars on the road, so I moved away from the roadside and walked along the broken white line down the middle.
Made me feel deliciously wicked. If Daddy could see me, he
would trace me off for walking in the road like that.

Daddy couldn't see me.

My throat was parched. I hoped Priithi had brought some
water from the standpipe in her yard. The taps in our house
weren't working.

When we had nothing else to do on those summer days, Priithi and I would go down to the train tracks and wait for passenger trains to pass. We'd wave at the people inside. Our hearts leapt when anyone waved back. It was as though, by them opening a hand to us, they were taking a little piece of us with them to wherever they were going, to exciting places we couldn't travel to.

The trains weren't coming right now, though.

Priithi was waiting for me by the gate to the playground. "You have everything?" she asked.

"For our hike? Yeah." I pointed to the rucksack on my back.

She craned her neck to look behind me. "Angela, it look like you scarcely fill it at all."

My face got hot, hotter than the sunshine warming it. "I did! I put in everything you said!"

"You put the matches?"

"Yes, but I only find half a box."

"Not even a lighter?"

I was so stupid. "I didn't think of that." Mummy kept a lighter in her purse. I should have gotten it out of there. It would only have been a little messy. "You want us to go back and get it?" I certainly wasn't going to go alone.

"Never mind," Priithi said. "We will manage."

"You bring water, Priithi? I so thirsty!"

She cut her eyes at me. "Of course not. You know you have to come and help me with it."

She was right. Water was heavy to carry, and we would need plenty of it for the two of us. "But I don't want to go to your house," I said.

"Coward."

"I just don't want to see. . . ."

"It not so bad," she replied. "Mostly dried up."

I took a deep, shaky breath and turned in the direction of Priithi's place. And, once again, she was right. The school was quiet, but then, people had stopped going there when it all started. The cows lying in the field across from the sweetie shop were like big, smelly raisins. There weren't as many flies buzzing around outside the shop like there had been before. So I guessed Mrs. Kramer who owned the shop was in the same shape as the cows. The people in the few cars along the roadside were quiet and still. Even Mummy had been almost dried up back at our house. I could have pried her hand off her handbag easy to get her lighter.

I should have realized when I smelled the something dead in the weeds; it was happening all over town. For the past month, everything had smelled like that, everywhere. The first symptom was dehydration. Then would come fever, bellyache, rage and violence, then getting quiet, lying down, deading, and drying up and floating away on the wind.

Priithi and I were going to walk our way out of town. In my rucksack, I had some stale bread, a can of condensed milk, and a roll of toilet paper. We would only need one roll, don't it? We wouldn't have to get very far. Don't someone would come and rescue us soon?

The sun was so hot! I rubbed my belly. I was getting vex. At everything, at everyone. Except Priithi.

If I concentrated really hard, I could feel Priithi's hand on my shoulder, guiding me to her house.

There was a rat lying by the roadside. Its legs were still moving a little bit. Something exploded in my mind. Screaming, I stomped it into pulp. The squishing and crunching under my sandals were almost as good as drinking cool water on a hot day. I scraped my sandals off along the ground and headed toward Priithi's place again.

It would be all right. When I got there, I just wouldn't look at her or her family, wherever they had each dropped down. I would just get some water from the standpipe; I wanted water so bad! Then maybe I would lie down for a little rest before I walked away from this town.

Repatriation

A few years ago, I was contracted to teach a writing workshop that was unable to access the space the organizer usually used. So she booked a block of berths on a Caribbean cruise, and held the workshop on board.

The workshop itself was great. Lots of fun, wonderful participants. But I'd never been on a cruise before, and I doubt I ever will again. Some of what I observed on board is in the story.

The coral-renewing technology used in the story is also real. It's called Biorock.™ It's cheap and effective, and was pioneered by Jamaican marine biologist Dr. Thomas Goreau and the late Dr. Wolf Hilbertz. Last I checked, it is not being used in Jamaica, though other countries with endangered coral reefs are instituting it.

INCREDULOUS, I looked up at the vast white steel bulk of the ship that was docked in the harbour. "A cruise, Jerry?" I said. "You really taking me on a *cruise* for my birthday?"

"Yes, Carlton. Stop fretting, nuh man? You going to like this one. I promise."

My husband had lost his goddamned mind. We both grew up as boys watching the cruise ships dock at our island, stinking the port up with the smell of tarry bunker fuel, disgorging tourists from foreign who would party for a few hours before jumping back on their traveling hotels for the next port of call. We would stare at them, our fingers clenched in the diamond-shaped holes of the chain-link fencing that prevented us locals from accessing our own port unless we were working for the cruise line and could show papers to prove it. Grew up witnessing the fierce competition for much-needed tourist dollars that encrusted the port: hundreds of stalls selling the same tired tat, cheap plastic dolls and brightly coloured clothing mass-produced in factories a-foreign and stamped with our country's name; the bars inside the protected cruise-ship zone where the drinks had cutesy names and DJs put on their best American accents to spin the same twelve pop songs that had had any reference to race or class edited out. *Play that funky music, bleep bleep.* So why the rass he thought I would want to join the Empire side of the Force for my fortieth birthday? Become one of those heedless, spendy foreigners who worked hard all year and just wanted a week of vacation with everything done for them? Who thought they were seeing the "real" Caribbean from their sheltered enclaves? Who kept parroting on about how beautiful the weather was, not seeing the pollution choking the harbour and the poverty and globalization choking the islands they visited?

I couldn't even hate them. They were just people, making what choices they could see in the belly of the same old shitsem beast that's devouring our planet. I hated what they represented.

Just because we were living a-foreign now didn't mean we were like them. We'd had to move to America because rising water levels and global warming were destroying our region, stealing health and hope and life. Didn't mean we had to parade around like . . .

Hang on. The people in the line all around us, waiting to go through the Florida Customs checkpoint to walk onto the ship. Their skins; black and brown like ours. Their voices; the same accent as ours. Their faces; alive with excitement, joy.

I tapped Jerry on the shoulder. "Wait. Where exactly we going?"

He smiled his secret smile. "You'll see. It's a surprise."

I hated surprises. He'd been making me grumpier with every passing week leading up to this birthday. Filling suitcase after suitcase with things he said we would need for this mysterious trip. Grabbing the mail from the mailbox before I could see it.

We were getting close to the front of the checkpoint, a bank of tall desks behind which people in uniforms looked down on the crowd, frowned at our papers, peered at our faces, asked intrusive questions, stamped our passports. The usual apprehension that came with crossing official American borders as a Black, gay man was making a knot in my belly. I fumbled in my wallet for my passport. "My ticket! Where's my ticket?"

Jerry patted my arm. "I have it, lover."

"But we each have to hold our own tickets and identification! That's how it always is!"

"Relax, nuh man?" Over my protests, he marched right up to the white-looking woman behind the desk, put both our tickets down on the desk in front of her, indicated me with his thumb, and said, "His fortieth birthday present. I trying to keep it secret as long as I can."

She favoured him with a generically stern gaze and reached an upturned palm to me, beckoning impatiently. "Come on. Your passport."

I handed it to her, made my smile friendly. She looked us both up and down, stared at our passport pictures, shone her little blue flashlight onto our tickets. I tried to see what destination was written on them, but Jerry leaned a little closer, blocking my view. She handed Jerry our documents and waved us past her to a row of X-ray machines.

I put my suitcase onto the conveyor belt. I took off my shoes and belt and put them there, too. I wondered, not for the first time, how many old Jewish people had PTSD flashbacks over that particular ritual. All around us, our fellow travelers were laughing and joking. I saw more than one large cardboard box bursting at the seams go through the scanner, held together by rolls and rolls of tape. You know when you live a-foreign, you haffe bring back plenty goods for the people back home when you going to visit. "Jerry? Where are all those suitcases you been filling up for the past month?"

He pecked my cheek. "Waiting for us in the hold. I sent them on ahead a few days ago."

Once we'd both made it through the scanner and facial recognition, I relaxed a bit. Before we moved on, I kissed him back. "I'm dying of curiosity," I said.

"Soon."

We and the other passengers bustled up a covered, switch-backed walkway, higher and higher, pulling/carrying/dragging our luggage with us. Pretty soon, I was breathing hard, thankful my suitcase was a hoverdeck that glided along behind me, keeping pace like a loyal dog. "This an exercise vacation?" I joked.

"You know me too love seeing you sweat."

The climb seemed endless, but it was probably only ten minutes later that we were on a long steel gangway beside the floating mountain that was the cruise ship. Up close, I could see its hull wasn't as pristine as it had first appeared. There were patches of rust here and there. Women and men in black slacks and short-sleeved white shirts greeted us and herded us along. "Welcome, welcome. Glad you're taking this beautiful trip with us." Seemed they all had our accent. I bristled at the benign reenactment of centuries of Black servitude, shame-faced at how comfortable I found it to be on its receiving end. As much to identify myself as a countryman as for the pleasure of it, I let myself relax into the familiar speech rhythms and manners of home as I returned the servers' greetings: "How do, Ma'am? Me? I deh-deh, you know how it is."

They checked our tickets, directed people to berths via eleva-tors and stairs fore and aft, port and starboard. Now Jerry and I were navigating a narrow corridor flanked by numbered doors of individual berths. Looked like the corridor used to be pan-eled. Now it was exposed steel piping, painted the same flaking white as the ship's hull. Jerry saw me frowning at it. He said, "So, there's this stuff called biorock."

"Sounds like a tween band from the Children's Television Network. Skin-teeth grins, watered-down street dance. Bad rap about the ABCs and not judging people by their looks."

"Wow. I can see you going to be big fun on this trip."

I was being an idiot. "Sorry, sorry."

The uniforms were different in this part of the ship. Now, every few metres we were greeted by a smiling brown person in black slacks and a Hawaiian-style shirt emblazoned with hula girls, coconut trees, and the name of the cruise line. I muttered to Jerry, "I just feel like I'm on a seagoing plantation."

"I know. It grinds my gears, too. I keep reminding myself that these people are employees, not slaves."

"A seagoing tourist resort, then."

"And we are in the twenty-first century, after all." He sighed. "At least they don't whip the help anymore."

"So why you bring us on this nightmare cruise, then?"

"I had a good reason. Soon tell you."

We'd reached our berth. The door scanned our faces, bonged a big red X on its screen facing Jerry, with an image of a dancing top hat. Jerry sucked his teeth impatiently. "To rass. They still can't make them smart enough to recognize someone wearing a hat?" He took off his baseball cap. The door rewarded him with a big green checkmark, tinnily chimed the notes of a soca tune, and clicked open for us. *Matilda, you take me money and gone with a bleep man.*

Our room was compact, clean, if the white sheets on the bed were a bit thin. We even had a sliding-glass door facing the ocean, and a little Juliet balcony we could step out onto.

We started unpacking.

The ship's horn sounded from outside, loud and deep as a kraken's call. The ship began slowly pulling out of port. Excited despite myself, I grinned at Jerry. I held my hand out to him. "Come for a walk on the main deck with me?"

Blasted ship was so big its main deck had streets. With names. And shops on those streets. Bakeries. Cafés. Jewellers. Pharmacies.

Something wasn't quite right, though. More than half the shops were closed and boarded up. And everything looked just a little bit, well, shabby. I said to Jerry, "This ship name *The Banana Boat*, or what? They keep the worst one in reserve for the Black people?"

"It will be better soon."

"Yeah? Something to do with the thing you were talking about—what it name? The prog rock?"

He chuckled. "You getting closer. They use it for building marine structures."

From far above our heads, speakers blared out two tones. "This is your captain, Hazel Joiner, speaking." I could hear the same message echoing from berths up and down the corridor. "Our cruising speed will top out at 30 knots to cover the distance of 964 nautical miles in just over a day. Please join me at eight bells—that's 8:00 p.m.—in the Admiralty Ballroom, where Chef Gaetan Boitano and his staff will be pleased to serve their last official meal here aboard the *Cetacean of the Seas* en route to Falmouth, Jamaica."

"Their last meal? The whole kitchen staff quitting en masse?"

"Biorock is a marvelous thing, you see?" He was leading me to an elevator. "Come. Up to the top deck." In the elevator, he continued, "If you put up a steel framework underwater, and run a light, harmless current through it, the current will unrust any rusty parts. Then the fence will go white from calcium deposits."

The view from the open upper deck was insane. Who puts three massive waterpark-style freshwater pools on a ship? With three-metre-tall water features in neon colours? Scores of children waded, screeching in glee, through them.

I looked at the vast pool deck, at the ocean below, rushing by at thirty knots per hour. "So much water, and they make a fake beach. No more beaches at the edge of Falmouth Town, though." Global warning brought super tornados, which had eroded the sand away. Polar ice-cap melts had raised water levels enough to permanently flood so many of our coastal cities.

There was a raised runway stage with an aerobics class in full progress on it, complete with boom-ch music issuing from the chest of the class instructor, one of the newest generation of nimble robots that could do parkour. No, not one of the newest. Every so often a rotor somewhere in its body jammed, and it got stuck for a second.

"Why we going Jamaica, Jerry, in this bucket of bolts? I thought cruise ships didn't land at Falmouth anymore?"

People reclined everywhere in deck chairs, while smiling staff brought them snacks and umbrella drinks.

He took me to the railing, as close to the bow as we could get. The giving sea, the killing sea, floated under and around us many storeys below. "After the electrical current lays down calcium on the steel frame," he told me, "coral and marine plants grow on it, faster and healthier than before. The coral resists bleaching, even if the water gets too warm. Oysters that grow on it are fat, their shells thick and healthy. Starfish stop melting."

"Starfish are melting now?" I asked, horrified.

A little boy careened past us, laughing to beat the band and chased merrily by a woman who looked to be his grandmother.

Jerry continued, "If you create a floating biorock reef in front of a dying one and an eroded beach, it will help filter pollutants out of the water. And it acts as a brake when storm surges come through. It mutes the wave action and deposits sand. It builds the beach back up, Carlton! New, clean beaches and coral reefs. Best part? It only takes months to see the difference. Scarcely a handful of years to restore the damage, clean the seas. We going to have Falmouth back!"

"We going on a working vacation, then?" I joked. "You going to have me laying down chicken wire in the slimy water outside Falmouth?"

He leaned out and pointed. His face was as lit with joy as those of our fellow passengers. "Look, Carlton." Stretched out in a diagonal line beside us was a row of rusting cruise ships, all heading the same way we were.

"Is what a gwan?" I asked.

"These ships all old," he replied. "Old steel. Time for them to get decommissioned now. When we disembark at Falmouth, the ships going to back off and moor just past the dead reef; the reef the cruise line pulverized in the first place to make a port here. They going to sink the ships to just below the water. And start running a harmless electrical current through them. You understand what happening now?"

I breathed in wonder. "They restoring the waters off Falmouth!"

"Yeah, man."

"But if our ship sink, how we going to get back?"

"I had everything we value packed into the hold. All these passengers did. Sweetie, we not on a cruise." Gently, he took me by the shoulders and turned me to face him. There were tears in his eyes. "If we want to stay, we can stay. We going home."

Sans Humanité

Basically, I collected a handful of weird images and anecdotes that had accumulated in my "ideas" files, put them into a blender, added connective tissue to the resulting glorp, and baked.

THE FIRST SYMPTOM is seeing dancing lights where none should be, or where, if you can reasonably expect to see lights— the night sky, for instance—they sure as shootin' shouldn't be twinkling and motivating and zipping around like kids on a playground. Stars are supposed to stay put.

Maybe it's more a sign than a symptom. I mean, if you've been working out for weeks and you suddenly realize that you can run up five flights of stairs without getting winded, is that a symptom? Or is it a sign that you're getting fitter?

The second symptom—sign—is a feeling of unreality that's difficult to explain. It doesn't happen constantly. Maybe you'll turn a corner on a familiar city street and see that abandoned old building from an angle you've never noticed before, and it just seems to *shine* somehow from within. It's not a creaky old death trap, dark inside with water-swollen joists and a grimy-sweet smell of rat piss, mould, and cockroach dung, but something more. Something otherworldly. And you'll get a feeling between your shoulder blades, as of wings unfurling. Or maybe your lover will turn their head to say something pretty mundane to you, like it's your turn to do the dishes, and even though there's no sunlight, the light will seem to stream through every molecule of their features. You'll be able to see every rich vein pulsing life life life under their skin, and they'll seem simultaneously fragile and ageless, and oh, so precious. You're beautiful, you'll say with tears in your eyes. And maybe they'll stop mid-mundanity and smile at you and give you a kiss. Or maybe they'll frown in irritation and say that's not going to get you out of doing the dishes. Or, thanks, dear, but I really gotta get going. Stupid meeting. Either way, the moment will have passed.

Sometimes those two signs come in reverse order.

The next one starts happening just as you're falling asleep. A voice calls your name soundlessly. It's a soft voice, one you know but can't quite place. It sounds tender, calming. You'll jolt awake. You know who that is. Do you? Your mother's voice? Your brother's?

You'll phone them and joke about how you're hearing them in your dreams. But what you really want to know is, are they okay? Did something happen? Are they afraid of something? Because you're beginning to wonder if you should be.

Then it gets into your dreams. Perfectly ordinary weird dreams, like your boss is wearing a tutu and selling pumpkins in front of the firehall. And you'll be la-la-la-ing along in dreamland, and then your boss turns her face to look at you, and it isn't her face at all, but a horrid dragonish version of it, skin pulled back so that you can see the bones beneath it, and her death-mask grin.

Next sign is seeing cities in the water. Or in the sky. Above your car, maybe. Or like that airline pilot whose plane was intercepted by a craft flying faster than any aeroplane can, and when it halted in the air in front of him, it was the size of a town, and he saw skyscrapers in it. That one's usually accompanied by electricity playing weird tricks. Hairs rising on your arms. Car lights flickering. Car coughing to a stop.

What comes after that? I don't know. No one does. What ever happened to that airline pilot, anyway? I'm not even sure what happened to me. I just woke and found myself here.

Upon the cold hillside . . .

And I'm calling your name. I can only reach you just as you're falling asleep. Please. It's me. I don't know where I am. Please come and get me.

Whimper

I have no idea what this story is about. It was written for the final issue of Black Clock Journal, *edited by Steve Erickson. To mark the occasion, Steve asked all the writers to name their stories either "Bang" or "Whimper," and to end in the middle of a sentence. I loved the concept.*

SHE RAN AND RAN through the undark nightlit city, crashing past parked cars and motorbikes, shoving between two raucous dressed-to-pussfoot women waiting in the line to get into Dutty Wine. They yelled hey and wha de rass as she broke through them. Smell of orange-blossom shampoo and musk perfume from the two of them glazed the inside of her nose. Screams from the Dutty Wine line as her leggobeast ploughed through it, questing tirelessly for her. She sped away from the sound. The sea was so close. Down that alley. She careened in that direction.

Her right footfront jammed up against something hard. Bright pain blossomed in her toes. Probably a flagstone jooking up out of the sidewalk. She couldn't take time to look down. She staggered in her purple plimsolls. Right knee made a crunk sound, collapsed a little outward. She felt the dislocation but not the pain from it. Made shift to stay on her feet, to runrunrun. Metallic quadruple thumps following behind her, repeated. She had to reach to the seawall, throw herself over the side. The air she sucked in sandpapered her throat, debrided her lungs. Her heart in her chest was a boiling kettle. Her open mouth the whistle. She pushed on down the alleyway, crumpled right knee now stabbing knives into her kneecap with every stride.

Leggobeasts-them couldn't abide sea water. People said so. Don't know which people, after nobody survived the touch of their leggobeast. Every hour of day nor night nowadays, the harbour full up of desperate bodies, only their heads showing as they bobbed on the oily water. Leggobeasts waited patiently at the water's edge until the person they were chasing gave up and swam back to be taken, or got too exhausted to swim and gave their lungs to the water. But she wouldn't. She wouldn't. If she could only reach before the leggobeast touched her.

She clattered through the alley, sobbing. Stumbled around a discarded mattress that reeked heavy of man piss. Sloshed through a reddish muddy liquid that smelled worse. Broken bottles crunched underfoot. And behind her, maybe only couple-three yards now, her personal leggobeast. Everybody had one. At least, is so people said. And when your time come, it going to get you, no matter what. Hers was an iron donkey. And tonight was her time. Her knee screamed with each step. But she moved. The clanking clatter sounded closer. Two yards? One? Her throat-hole was on fire. She broke out of the alleyway, hooves thumpity thump behind her, near enough to throw the shadow of an equine muzzle over her shoulder and onto the ground. Flat dark sea in front of her across the two-lane highway. Only things between her and the water: light traffic and the low metal restraining wall. Ranged out all along the narrow lip of soil between the sea wall and the sea; silhouettes of leggobeasts. Each one different.

No time. People had it to say that only the touch of your personal leggobeast would kill you; you were safe from all the others. She dodged cars, blowing panic and pain through her lips. Threw herself over the side of the restraining wall. Limped to the edge. Pushed between two of the shadows. One had deep rough fur and rank breath. They breathed? The other felt like tree bark.

She let herself fall into the water. A floret of bubbles bloomed upward around her as she plunged down. She stroked, pushing for the air above. She tried to kick, but her knee screamed at her. She broke the surface and kept swimming away from the shoreline as quickly as she could. She wasn't a good swimmer. The water might as well have been molasses.

"Ow!"

Her hand had smacked someone in the head. "Sorry," she hissed through clenched teeth.

"Beg pardon."

"Is all right," the other woman replied. "Just go easy. Plenty of we in here."

Treading water—though not with the bad leg—she looked around. Her sight had adjusted to the dark. Yes, heads bobbing everywhere, all staring back at their leggobeasts onshore. She swiveled herself around in the water to face hers. "Why nobody swimming away?" she asked the woman beside her.

"Swimming to go where?"

She hadn't thought it through that far. "To a ship?" The harbour was strangely empty.

A man not too far off said, "Once you on the ship, you not in water any more. Your leggobeast will just materialize and take you." His voice was hoarse.

"How long you been in the water?" Sea salt was already making her lips pucker. He replied, "I don't know. Maybe two days? I can't hold on a lot longer."

Voices called out from the darkness: one day; one hour; don't remember how long; so hungry. A man with bloodshot eyes said, "My own show up this afternoon. Been waiting for 'im. I throw two good bullets in 'im rass from my gun. The shots land, but the bullet holes close right over."

The woman she'd bumped into—who was now dog-paddling slow circles around her—asked, "Which one is yours?" She jutted her chin toward the shore line.

"The shiny one." Her leggobeast had taken its place in the lineup. It was perched, delicately as a hill-climbing goat, on the shallow ledge of land. It looked at her, she was sure of it. It stamped one foot. The air and water were so still, she could hear its bolts rattle.

The woman said, "Look my own yah-so. Three over from yours, to the right."

"The one that look like a tree?"

"A cashew tree, in fact. With a child's face embedded in the trunk."

Something touched her shoulder. She jerked away from it and yelled out before she saw what it was. A length of wooden plank, not yet waterlogged. She grabbed it, gratefully let it take some of her weight. She called out, "I find a piece of wood. Allyuh want to share?"

"Yes, please, lady, do!"

"And me!"

Pretty soon, five of the floaters were clinging to the length of branch, with the rest holding onto their ankles. Had been six of them, but one disappeared as soon as he touched the wood. On the shore the structure that had looked like a crumbling old shack disappeared at the same time. She'd forgotten: that was a leggobeast, too. Soon they had a third row of people clinging to the people clinging to the five. They all starfished out on the surface of the water.

She said to the woman who first spoke to her, "How come the plank didn't disappear when the leggobeast took that guy?"

"Don't know. I really have to pee." The water between her and the woman got warm for a few seconds, then cooled off again. "Sorry."

"Don't fret." They all floated in silence awhile. From the horizon a wash of blue crept up the sky. On the shore, her iron donkey reared. It thrust its muzzle to the sky, came down with a clank and a rattling of bolts.

"Yours talk to you?" the young woman asked.

"Only in my dreams."

"I used to dream about mine, too. That's how I knew it was coming."

She called out, more to make conversation than because she really wanted to know, "Allyuh not thirsty? And how you shit?"

"We do it right ya so, lady. The sea does carry it away."

The sea salt was burning her lips. She started to moisten them with her tongue. Thought of what she was floating in. Spat instead. She didn't have plenty to spit with; her mouth was nearly dry. "And how you eat?"

"We don't . . ."

"I see one boy. He get tired waiting for death. He swim right back up to his leggobeast. Grabbed its ankle. It took him."

She said, "You know what I wonder?"

Someone replied, "What?"

"How we so sure is a bad thing for our leggobeasts to fetch us away?"

"How you mean, how? Is obvious, nuh?"

"No, think—maybe they take us to something better than this. Well, of course better than this right here. But I mean, your lives before your leggobeast—what those were like?"

Thereafter came a litany of joys and woes: a good job; a dying husband; a call from a long-lost friend; fifty dollars found between the couch cushions; poverty; prosperity; failed exams; cancer diagnoses. And the guy who admitted having just shot his best friend. The rest edged away from him, spoiling the symmetry of the starfish. He sobbed. They watched. Snot glistened on his upper lip. He wailed, "I so sorry, Robbie!" The sobs crested, then fell off. The man let go his hold on the person who was supporting him and floated, spinning in a slow circle. No one moved to stop him. On the shore a gelid lump, man-high, disappeared. So did the murderer's body. She couldn't see how he had died.

"See?" said the woman, her new friend in adversity. "That's how we know is a bad thing to let your leggobeast catch you. Even if they don't touch you, when you dead, they go, too. So they nuh must mean death?"

"And that's a bad thing?" The gonging pain in her knee was almost background noise, a spike being driven over and over again into her cold-numbed leg. One of the starfish arms was holding that ankle, but she barely noticed.

"So," said the young woman. "You didn't answer your own question." She went silent. She didn't want to do this.

But the woman persisted. "What your life was like? Something to stay for, or to run from?"

She swallowed. "I running from the end of the world."

"Of course is the end. One of those things for every human on the planet. How running going to help?"

"I need to stop it. 'Cause is me who start it."

Murmurs from around and behind her. A voice said, "You? How you coulda do this?" Someone else said, "Is not she. Is aliens."

Someone else ventured, "Messengers of God."

She said, "No. Is me. I dream them."

The youth across from her: "We all dream them. Is that make we know we number come up."

She replied, "I dream all of them. Every single one. Before this ever start. Dream them by the score. Dream armies of them. I still dreaming them. Six billion of them is a lot of dreaming." No one said anything. The sky had lightened to foreday morning, enough for her to make out their stunned expressions. She pointed to the shore. "That one there? With all those foot-long teeth? I dream he last year. Looking exactly so. I dream the one that take away the Prime Minister last month." She pointed farther down the line. "That one that could be a little girl in her frilly princess dress, except she have too many legs? I dream she. The bruk-down house this plank come from? I dream it last night. Same time I dream my own."

Someone made a small, sad noise.

"That duppy girl with the plenty foot is my one. You really send that thing after me? You send them after alla we?"

The creatures were starting to shuffle and shift about un-
easily where they stood. Oh, God. She knew what was coming. "I didn't do it on purpose!" she yelled. "I tried to stop! But
how you going to hold back your dreams?"

"I know a way," said a voice. A hand gripped the back of
her neck and shoved her beneath the water. She stopped up her
breath and struggled, but the hand was too strong. There was
commotion all around her, legs kicking. Were they trying to help
her, or to help drown her? She wished she could stop fighting,
let herself die. Had been wishing it since this all started.

The implacable hand was still holding her down. Her lungs
bellowed, airless. From underneath, the surface of the water
was a refractive lens. It let her see all the leggobeasts in their
long line at the edge of the sea. Spots floated in front of her eyes.
She tried to stop struggling, but her body wouldn't give up. Her
mind, though, was thinking quickquickquick. Do it quick.
Because last night, her dreams had changed. The leggobeasts
had changed. Even as she couldn't hold her breath any longer,
opened her mouth and sucked killing brine into herself, she
watched the leggobeasts.

Together, moving as one, they floated a few feet up into
the air. As she twisted and drowned, she saw the leggobeasts,
each flying toward their person. Her iron donkey was in the air
above her, starting to descend toward her. She hadn't told the
young woman, she remembered. Hadn't told her what the iron
donkey said in her dre

Propagation: A Short Story

Some years ago, author Neil Gaiman was tapped by TED (the organization that produces the TED talks) to curate an evening of storytelling at its annual conference in Vancouver, Canada, with Amanda Palmer as MC. The authors who said yes to Neil's invitation were Sofia Samatar, Monica Byrne, Nnedi Okorafor, and me. TED wanted optimistic science fiction stories from us. I often find that a difficult order, because I vaguely resent being constrained to be "positive." So the story was fighting me the whole way. As I was about to hop on the plane from Southern California to Vancouver to give the reading that same evening, it occurred to me that I hadn't confirmed the validity of the scientific premise of my story. I quickly left a message for an old friend of mine to whom I often turn when it's a question of biology. I arrived at my Vancouver hotel a few hours later to a message from him. As I'd feared, the science not only didn't but couldn't work. I had mere hours to do something. I went blank with panic for a few seconds, then I implored my outside-the-box ADHD brain to work its magic for me.

It did. It reminded me why I very much wanted the story to turn out the way it did, why it felt vital to locate its hope for future possibility in the experience of a poor, young, inner-city Black girl from the Caribbean. It reminded me that strict science fictional protocols and narratives that presume cultural ownership of the means of technological progress often don't quite fit stories told from the perspective of marginalized communities. (If only because the realities of our lives and histories under colonialism are so beyond belief that sometimes we needs must have recourse to the metonymizing possibilities of the fantastic in order to tell our stories.) It reminded me that in order for us to have futures, the impossible needs to be made possible. It reminded me that that's what science fiction does. It reminded me that speculative fiction often plays fast and loose with genre norms. And it reminded me that the story needed to serve me, not the other way around. I could mess with form as much as I wished in order to tell my story.

I took a deep breath and began reinventing the piece. Halfway through, Neil called my hotel room. As if to prove that he knows me better than I think, he apprehensively asked me whether my piece would be ready. (Or maybe he's just psychic. God, I hope not.) I promised him that it would. Because by then, I'd begun to get the feeling that, incredibly, it would, with only minutes to spare until I had to leave for the event.

What I came up with was part fiction, part essay, all performance piece. It was a largely fantastical examination of scientific progress and what it needs to do to benefit the whole world, not just certain populations.

When I gave the reading, the audience seemed to very much enjoy it. Neil pronounced himself satisfied. He understood what the story was trying to do. And I was relieved.

Here's the rub: when you read this story as words on a page, it doesn't gel. I've had people both read it and then see me do it. For them, it only clicks when delivered as a piece of performative speculative storytelling, with commentary, told in multiple, code-switching registers. For me, that means it returns to my roots in Caribbean orature. And I'm happy with that. Very happy.

Just don't tell Neil I was still writing it when he called.

ONCE UPON A TIME one fore day morning, a loud bang wake Kinitra and her young brother Purvis from off them mash-up mattress on the floor in the corner of the one room where Kinitra and Purvis and Ma and Grandma all of them living.

Grandma was sitting in the rocking chair by the window. Same place she was sitting when Kinitra go to bed last night.

The noise make Ma sit up in her and Grandma's bed. The white nightie and the darkness in the room make Ma brown skin look black, true black. She tell Purvis and Judith to hush them bloodcloth mouth is probably just them blasted shottas again with them born-fi-dead stupidness like the battle them was waging with the rasscloth police all through the dungle last night wasn't enough for them, ee?

Grandma say is not shottas, daughter. Been sitting here all night, you know how the old bones don't need plenty rest. Nobody outside. Shottas and all gone to bed hours ago.

Fore day morning light coming in the window was enough for Kinitra to see Grandma look at her, hard. Not enough to see what kind of mind Grandma was examining her with. Grandma know her granddaughter good, for Kinitra had a suspicion the noise that just shake the whole of the dungle was her fault.

Ma say, "Me never know gun to sound like that. Just one boom, and loud so?"

Purvis had already run straight to Grandma. She pull him onto her wide lap. She lie his head against her breast. Time was, that would have been Kinitra taking comfort in her grandmother's arms. But she was too big now. Time to take action instead.

There was another sound, soft on the tinning roof over them heads. "Is rain that?" Ma asked.

"In dry season?" Grandma reply.

Little Purvis gasp, him y'eye-them big as him look out the window. "Feathers!"

Grandma screw up her eyes to try to see is what him a-chat bout. She couldn't see too good any more. Old bones, old eyes.

Kinitra ongle asking herself what went wrong. Bird feathers? Couldn't be. So she too get out of bed and go over to the window. Not Ma. Ma all the time saved her strength for the necessaries; walking to work at the factory in the morning before bus start run, working at the factory, taking the bus home from the factory come evening, doing the same thing the next day, six days a week.

Kinitra look out the window. Wasn't feathers raining from

the sky, landing pop-pop-pop on the roof, filling the air with the warm smell of—

"Popcorn!" Kinitra's heart swell up in her throat. She didn't dare laugh, for she wasn't ready yet to confess what she had been getting up to. She just watch the white fluff drifting down onto the dungle. Popcorn. Like Grandma make sometimes, shaking the kernels in the big pot on the stove with the kibber shut tight. Hot popcorn cook with coconut oil and afterwards some salt and a little pat of margarine on top afterwards. Butter when they could afford it.

Brother Purvis looked up at Kinitra. "Popcorn? Heaven popcorn?"

Grandma laugh when she hear that. She gie Purvis a big kiss on the cheek for being a clever boy. Ma even get out of her bed to come see the heaven corn. Couple-few popcorns had landed on the window ledge. Ma picked one up and sniff it. She frown. Put a single popcorn onto her tongue, like a communion wafer. Kinitra hold her breath, 'fraid say her food would make her ma sick. She was just about to beg Ma to spit the popcorn out, but Ma swallow. She smile. "It good."

Grandma try it too, but she ongle say, "Huh." You know the way grandmothers stay. Kinitra had to squabble with Purvis for the pieces remaining on the window sill. Purvis ask Ma if he could go outside and eat more. Ma say shottas could still be dey-bout, but she let Purvis open the door little way and stick his hand out the door bottom and collect some handsful of popcorn. Ma inspect each piece and throw 'way any piece that had even a speck of dungle dirt on it.

As the sun was coming up, for a few minutes the ground of the dungle was white like a duppy-dead, instead of warm red dirt and the grey of pavement and mash-up asphalt road and little strokes of living green swips swips all over the place of weeds growing through the broken pavement.

Kinitra had her business to see to. She was dying to get up onto the roof, but she couldn't do it under Ma's johncrow eye, quick to spy out any mischief. So Kinitra say, "Grandma, what time it is?"

Grandma pick up her cell phone from the window sill. "Six thirty-two." Then she say to Ma, "Carol, nuh time for you to go to work?" Then she wink at Kinitra. That's how Kinitra know that Grandma's mind was favouring her in this business.

Ma grumble 'bout how toil never done. But she onned the lights. She went in the bathroom and cleaned herself with the water remaining in the bathtub. She put on her work clothes. She fill a yogurt container with some leftover peas and rice and stew chicken from the fridge. She remind Purvis and Kinitra of their Saturday chores: Purvis to fetch water from the standpipe out in the road so Kinitra could cook and mop the floor and so the women of the house could bathe decent in the tub, not half-naked by the standpipe like the dungle men and boys.

It was sun-up and by now, the whole dungle knew is what a-gwan, how the heavens open up and rain food like manna down 'pon them. It was commotion in the streets. People fetching up popcorn in bucket and cup. And the wonderful smell, Lawd Jesus. The smell of hot coconut oil and exploded corn kernels. The whole time Ma giving them instructions, Purvis sidling over to the door, ready to run get his share. Kinitra ongle fighting herself not to look up at the ceiling. The big bang, it come from their roof. She had to go check on the Mole. If it break, she nah know how to get another one.

Finally, *finally* Ma leave for work. Purvis dash outside with their bucket. Grandma shout after him that he best fill that bucket up with clean water, not snacks from off the ground. Then she turn to Kinitra. "Is you do this?"

"I think so. I didn't mean for it to turn out so. I don't know what happen."

"Well go then, nuh?" Grandma waved Kinitra toward the stairs behind the apartment. "Go see to your precious assembler."

You haffe understand, Kinitra's Ma had plenty reason not to check for the gangs and their shottas. She could lose her boy pickney to them any day now, and her girl pickney in worse ways. Already lost her baby brother to them ten years previous. Kinitra's Uncle Selvon was still living, but some of the things he had to do to stay that way, he wouldn't or couldn't discuss.

Time was, drug trade was a big—Uncle would say "income stream" in gang business. But when it get to where any puss or dog could build them own 3D printer and print out as much cocaine as them want, well, the gangs had to diversify. Uncle Selvon's gang went into politics—what Ma would call "politricks"—and Uncle Selvon give Kinitra them old 3D printer, 'cause he know say him young niece like feh passa-passa with all kind of machine.

Okay, here's the thing; this story doesn't work. The science in it isn't science. For text-based science fiction, that's a real problem. As a general rule, the science and technology in our stories have to be plausible, or at the very least, convincing. I've confirmed with my favourite geneticist that the science in my story as I'm currently conceiving it is a dud.

Duds will become important later.

When I realized my story was dying on vine, as it were, I tried a bunch of things. I changed the premise a bit. No go. I moved on to one of my other story ideas; I have quite a few of them. Nope, that didn't work either.

Then an interesting thing happened: Nnedi and I were at a conference a few days ago where we learned from a frustrated artist who's been in the media business for decades that some producers at the top of the entertainment food chain still believe that Black people have no interest in science and science fiction, and that we are incapable of envisioning ourselves having a place in the future. All of us. Therefore, these producers refuse to greenlight any science fiction projects aimed at Black audiences.

When African American science fiction author Walter Mosley—he also writes in many other genres—considered the question of what use science fiction is to Black people, he said that we, like so many other people in the world, need to be living in a different world. And in order to figure out how to get there, we need to be able to imagine what that world might be.

The lovely thing about the fiction of the fantastic is that through it, we can imagine the realities we want to see in the world. We can imagine pathways to getting there. So, reality be damned. I'm going to tell you the story I would write if I could. It's a Caribbean fairy tale or tall tale of science and technology. It couldn't possibly happen this way; I'm not going to try to convince you that it could. In the spirit of figuring out what we want from the world if we're to have any hope of putting our heads together and making that world:

A few years from now, not very long, a young girl named Kinitra will be living in a Caribbean island nation, in a rundown area of its capital city. The area where Kinitra will live is called the "Dungle." Some people say the word "dungle" come from "dunghill." Me nah know for sure, but me could tell you is the kind of place Desmond Dekker was talking about when he sang,

"Dem a-loot / Dem a-shoot / Dem a-wail / In Shanty Town."

Plenty of hardscrabble people living in the dungle. Plenty of gangs. Nuff shottas some nights, shooting up the place with their born-feh-dead wars. For although is the future, you know how bad things can take a long time to change, right? Good things usually temporary, but bad things have staying power.

Uncle Selvon love 'im niece Kinitra plenty plenty. In this not-too-future time, Uncle Selvon will give Kinitra one old discarded 3D printer. At first, Kinitra will collect the throw-way plastic that her city drowning in and use it to print out plates and bowls for their kitchen. But after a while, Ma will tell Kinitra that ongle four people living in this house. Them nah need no more plate and bowl. So Kinitra will try to print comfortable shoes for Ma's aching feet. Ongle the plastic make Ma's feet sweat in the tropical sun. The sweat would gather up into the plastic shoes-dem till Ma's feet slide around so much on the shoe bottom that she swear say her feet swimming in their own salty ocean. Besides, Grandma say some of that plastic not so healthy for putting against their bodies, or for eating peas and rice and stew oxtail out of. Or anything else, for that matter.

So Kinitra will start to fiddle with the printer. It will tek her some time. She will beg her Uncle Selvon bring her all kinda parts and chemicals. She will be forever using Grandma's data plan to Google principles of molecular assembly on Grandma's cell phone. Yes, I know; the level of computer programming and modeling she going to need to absorb will be *crazy*! But

give any little girl or boy half a chance, and them will surprise
you. As to the equally insane amounts of raw power her Mac-
Guffin will require, I going to leave that to developments in
miniaturization, the use of quantum power, and what have
you. To help her along, our world going to have to figure out
how to get cheap, reliable power to a little shantytown girl
whose house don't have running water or reliable electricity.

Finally Kinitra will find a way to marry a 3D printer with a
molecular assembler. Finally she will realise that if smaddy can
build an assembler, them nah can get it to disassemble, too?

In this-ya tall tale, Kinitra will know exactly what she want
to make first; corn. On the cob. Something her Ma love like
puss love to purr. She will ask Grandma where she could find
carbon and oxygen to feed little Mole.

Grandma will think about it. "From the air?" she reply to
Kinitra. "According to how that is what air mek from."

Kinitra will get likkle bit of organic raw materials from, say,
roadkill, grass clippings, seaweed, the colloidal swamp of trash
floating in the sea like a beard around the industrial and densely
populated parts of the island, and so forth.

But she one won't be able to collect all that, not even with
her brother and Grandma helping. Point is, after her Mole disassemble all the raw materials into separate hoppers—tens of
thousands of them! I know, it's impossible!—then it would be
easy for her to assemble the components into anything, organic
or inorganic.

I don't know about you, but whenever I see the Mickey
Mouse animated version of *The Sorcerer's Apprentice*, where the
apprentice is punished for using his master's technology to
create an automatic broom that will replicate itself endlessly,
sweeping the whole time, I think, poor Caliban Mouse. Trying

to use Massa's tools, but Massa nah go let you refabricate 'im house. The lesson I'm supposed to learn from that story is that power will never share itself. I have to believe that's not always true.

At first, Kinitra won't tell Ma about her corn-making plans, for Ma would worry about her gyal pickney passa-passa-ing with chemical reactions that could release the bonds that hold this Earth where we living in a form that can sustain us.

Kinitra going to set the Mole up on the roof and turn it on. You know what happen next. She won't have the heat or quantity settings right, so when she activate little Mole, it make too much corn, then overheat so bad it cause popcorn day in the dungle. Is so fairy tales go; the heroine have to try three times, fail disastrously the first two. The second time she try, little Mole run out of ingredients too fast. So it source more it own self, by collecting waste from our skies and our waters. How to prevent this from becoming a "grey goo" disaster scenario, where out-of-control nanobots replicate exponentially, devouring everything living and non to make more nanobots? Me nah know, Star. But for the sake of the young daughter, for the sake of us all, lewwe try, seen?

But for the pickneys in the dungle, that first day will be the famous day, the day popcorn fall free from the sky like rain till popcorn was ankle-deep on the ground, and them eat till them tired fill them belly full with it, so then they started pelting each other with it, running and laughing through the streets of the dungle.

This is how the story end, like most stories, with a beginning: some of the popcorn kernels will be duds. Them didn't pop. And clearly didn't get overheated, for one day, Kinitra will discover that they sprouting all through the dungle.

Yes, you probably thinking the same thing I thought; if she's learned to engender life, that makes her a god. And I have to tell you, nothing plays more havoc with fiction than gods. All that omnipotence; them jus' a-change up the plot all the time to suit them own self, and then there goes your readers' suspension of disbelief. But I choose to understand Kinitra's creation of life at the level of fable and allegory. Canadian children's writer Robert Munsch experienced censorship of his picture book *The Giant, or Waiting for the Thursday Boat* when he dared to depict God as a little brown girl. But when I look into the eyes of children, I often see divinity. It's in the eyes of female or poor or disabled or trans or queer or brown children, too. I choose to fantasize about a world where they don't receive daily messages telling them they are less than beasts. I choose to dream of a world in which a little Black girl can take some dud corn and use it to heal the world.

Nalo Hopkinson was born in Kingston, Jamaica, and also spent her childhood in Trinidad and Guyana before her family moved to Toronto, Canada, when she was sixteen.

Hopkinson's novels include *Brown Girl in the Ring, Midnight Robber, The Salt Roads, The New Moon's Arms, The Chaos,* and most recently, *Sister Mine.* She has edited four anthologies, including *Whispers from the Cotton Tree Root: Caribbean Fabulist Fiction* and the British Fantasy Award–winning *People of Colo(u)r Destroy Science Fiction!* anthology coedited with Kristine Ong Muslim. She was the lead author of *House of Whispers,* a serialized comic in Neil Gaiman's *Sandman Universe.*

In 1997, Hopkinson won the Warner Aspect First Novel Contest for *Brown Girl in the Ring. Brown Girl in the Ring* was also nominated for the Philip K. Dick Award and received the John W. Campbell and Locus Awards for Best First Novel. Her collection *Skin Folk* received the World Fantasy

Award and the Sunburst Award for Canadian Literature of the Fantastic. *The Salt Roads* received the Gaylactic Spectrum Award for positive exploration of queer issues in speculative fiction. *The New Moon's Arms* won the Sunburst Award, making Hopkinson the first author to receive the award twice, and Canada's Prix Aurora Award. In 2020, Hopkinson was named the 37th Damon Knight Grand Master by the Science Fiction Writers of America, the youngest and the first woman of African descent to receive this lifetime honour.

Her fantasy novel *Blackheart Man* is forthcoming from Saga Press in August 2024. She is also collaborating as script writer with artists John Jennings (*I Am Alfonso Jones*) and Stephen Bissette (*The Swamp Thing*) on *Night Comes Walking*, a horror graphic novel forthcoming from Megascope, an imprint of Abrams ComicArts.

Hopkinson was one of the founders of the Carl Brandon Society, which exists to further the conversation on race and ethnicity in speculative fiction. As a Professor of Creative Writing at the University of California, Riverside, she was a member of a research cluster in science fiction and of the University of California's "Speculative Futures Collective." She has been a Writer-in-Residence a number of times at both the Clarion Workshop in San Diego, California, and Clarion West in Seattle, Washington. She is currently a professor in the School of Creative Writing of the University of British Columbia in Vancouver, Canada.

NISI SHAWL (they/them) is the multiple award–winning author, coauthor, and editor of more than a dozen books of speculative fiction and related nonfiction, including the standard text on diverse representation in literature, *Writing the Other: A Practical Approach*; the Nebula Award–finalist novel *Everfair*; the first two volumes of the *New Suns* anthology series; and the Aqueduct Press short story collection *Filter House* (co-winner of the 2009 Otherwise Award).

Shawl is a founding member of the Carl Brandon Society and a member of the Clarion West Writers Workshop Board of Directors. They've spoken at Duke University, Spelman College, Stanford University, Sarah Lawrence College, and many other learning institutions.

Recent titles include a new, horror-adjacent story collection from Aqueduct Press, *Our Fruiting Bodies*; the middle-grade historical fantasy novel *Speculation*, published by Lee & Low;

and *Kinning,* their book-length sequel to *Everfair,* an excerpt of which is available on the Tor/Forge blog. "Sun River," a short story sequel to *Everfair,* appeared in 2023 on Reactor, formerly the Tor.com site.

About the Cover Artist

JOSHUA MAYS is a Denver-born painter, illustrator, and muralist. His murals include the BEACON series, found across Oakland, California, and his illustrations have been featured in Jill Scott's collection *The Moments, the Minutes, the Hours.*

Mays studied illustration at the Community College of Denver before moving to Philadelphia. He has created commissions in Washington, DC; Denver; Portland, Oregon; Philadelphia; London; Johannesburg; Mexico City; and Jakarta. He also collaborates with other artists, such as Eric Okdeh and King Britt, for the Mural Arts Philadelphia's Art Education program.

Mays currently lives in Oakland, California.